The Bitter Harvest

From the tales of Orenda

Gray Door Ltd.

Copyright © 2016 Oliver Phipps. All rights reserved.

ISBN 978-0-9908034-9-2

Table Of Contents

Chapter One: In the Company of Warriors
Chapter Two: A Desperate Place
Chapter Three: Vicious Encounter
Chapter Four: Nazshoni's Story
Chapter Five: Trapping Devils
Chapter Six: Blood Song
Chapter Seven: Bad to Worse
Chapter Eight: A Tear for the Brave
Chapter Nine: Black Eyes of Death
Chapter Ten: Storm Rider
Tears of Abandon
Chapter One: A Daring Plan
Chapter Two: Whisper
Twelve Minutes till Midnight
Ghosts of Company K
Diver Creed Station
Where the Strangers Live
The House on Cooper Lane
Bane of the Innocent

The Bitter Harvest

Chapter One: In the Company of Warriors

Onsi moved nervously through the busy rendezvous, leading his horse amongst a maze of Native American traders mixed with white fur trappers and merchants. He pulled in a breath of the damp air. It was a fine spring morning of 1825. The frontier gatherings were wisely held in the prime of the year for the purpose of buying and selling goods.

The young man's senses were stimulated by a variety of sights, smells, and sounds he'd rarely been exposed to. He stopped and gazed out over the vast area, searching for the person of his quest.

"Good morning Chief. You seem to be looking for something; I've just the thing for you."

A white tradesman in weathered gentleman's apparel stirred the young man from his endeavor. Onsi turned and looked at the man who was staring intently at him and holding a small bottle in his hands.

"I'm not a chief." He replied to the white man with accented English.

"Yes, well, you seem to be searching for something, and I think I can help you."

As he said this the man once again raised the small bottle, as if to display it for the young man.

"Thank you, Sir; I'm searching for the Great Warrior. Can you help me find him? I've been told he would be here. He travels with his wife and her brother."

The white tradesman appeared puzzled by the man's question. He considered it briefly and then replied slowly.

"The Great Warrior? You must mean David Crockett."
Onsi appeared confused.
"David, who?" he asked.
The small bottle lowered a little in the man's hands. "Davy Crockett. The Great Warrior. He killed a bear when he was just a lad."
Onsi again thought about this for a few seconds.
"A bear... the warrior I'm searching for has killed a Skadegamutc."
The whiter trader expressed complete confusion, "A what?"
"A Skadegamutc, uhm... a big, uhm, terrible... ah, what you call... a demon?"
Now the small bottle and the trader's hands lowered all the way down as he stared at the young man with disbelief.
"A demon, I don't know of any warrior like that."
Just then, the young man noticed something in the distance. He motioned with his hand in a thankful gesture.
"Thank you, it's all very well. I see now what I've been searching for. Thank you."
As Onsi lead his horse away, the trader remembered his initial thought.
"Yes, well you might also be interested in this miracle elixir! It cures everything; you won't find it anywhere else on the frontier."
Onsi paid no attention to the tradesman as he moved cautiously towards his objective.
A ways off and across a muddy trail he spotted a young man and also a young woman. Both sat on horses and both had a pack horse connected to their own. The woman held the reins of a large beautiful horse as well, which indicated another rider was close by. Onsi immediately realized that only a man of importance could afford such things as these.

He maneuvered around the two and as he could see them better, he was certain they matched the descriptions of the people he'd been searching for.

The woman appeared to be in her early twenties. She was very beautiful and seemed to be Cherokee. The young man beside her also appeared to be Cherokee and looked like the woman's younger brother.

Onsi found an inconspicuous location to wait. He then began to search for the warrior. As he was looking around, a white trapper staggered up to the woman. He appeared to have drunk too much of the white man's drink called "whiskey," and now, he examined the young woman with obvious desire.

"Hello there. You're sure a pleasant sight for a man that hasn't seen a woman for months." The white trapper spoke with slurred speech.

The roughly dressed man came closer to the young woman's leg. Her buckskin dress was pulled high due to the way she sat in the saddle, and this caused much of her legs to be exposed.

The man carefully looked at her leg.

"You Indian women do like to show them pretty legs of yours don't cha."

The young woman stared down at the man who was slowly moving closer to her leg. She said nothing but moved her right hand over to the handle of a knife in her leather moccasin boot. She pulled the knife out slightly as she glanced over to her brother. He also watched the man with obvious irritation.

"Do you mind if I just touch that pretty leg a little? I just want to touch it once."

He looked up to the woman who gazed down at him without expression, as her horse moved slightly under her.

Onsi had now become very interested in this development and almost forgot about the warrior he was searching for. Then a large native man came out from the trader's tent in front of the young man and woman. He was around thirty years old, very distinguished in appearance and was examining a musket in his hands as if he'd just traded for the long gun.

By this time, the rough trapper was rubbing the woman's exposed leg. She turned her head up and looked at the large man with the musket. He glanced up from the weapon in his hands and realizing a man was beside her; he began to take notice.

The woman spoke softly in a mix of native languages and asked the man with the musket, "May I kill him?"

The large man couldn't see that the trapper was rubbing her leg, due to her brother's horse.

The man with the musket answered her casually, in the same mix of native languages that was used for trading. Onsi understood what he said, but it was apparent the white fur trapper didn't understand this language.

"No, I don't believe it would be wise. He's just got too much crazy white man juice in him."

Then the woman's brother intentionally moved his horse back a little. This allowed the large man to see that the white trapper was rubbing the woman's leg.

The large man's face became stretched with anger. He stared at the man as if barely containing himself. Then he told the woman, "You may remove a finger if you wish."

Onsi was astounded by this and watched the following events unfold within a few short seconds.

The woman still held her knife. As the large man told her she could remove a finger, the white trapper turned around, seeming to realize the woman spoke to someone behind him. He smiled at the large man and raising his hand from the woman's leg, pointed up to her and asked, "Is this here yer woman?"

The Bitter Harvest

At the very instant the man pointed to her with his head turned, the woman pulled her knife, sliced off the trapper's finger with one quick movement. Before he'd realized she had removed his finger, the young woman was cleaning the blade on the horse's blanket and putting it back into her leather moccasin boot.

The white trapper, feeling something hit his hand, turned to see blood oozing from where his finger had just been. Shock spread across his face. He began to moan as the pain took hold. He reached up with his other hand and held the wounded one in dismay.

Now the large man walked over to him. He took the man by his coat and moved him away from the horses. Then he spoke to the man in broken English.

"You've lost a finger today. But you're fortunate to have your life yet. She could have removed your head just as easily."

He then looked around to make sure no one was close by. He turned back to the man who was still staring wide eyed at his hand. With one quick movement, the large man head-butted the trapper, who stumbled back and fell into the muddy path, completely unconscious.

Onsi stepped back a bit more into his hiding spot but possessing few doubts that this was the man he'd traveled far to find.

The large man placed the musket into the ropes of a pack horse, and after climbing on his own, they rode casually away.

A few moments later Onsi mounted his horse and followed at a distance.

The three slowly rode west. Only the sounds of the horses and surroundings were heard as they moved along barely visible trails.

After about two hours, the woman's brother stopped. The large man and the woman soon stopped as well. They looked back and then turned their horses and returned to him.

All three held their mounts steady for a short time. Then the large man spoke softly, "One rider."

The woman's brother nodded and added, "This rider has been following us since the traders gathering. He's traveling too light for a warrior. I think this rider is a messenger."

The large man and the woman again remained silent as if listening. Then the large man began to turn his horse; he replied, "It seems we'll have a guest for our late meal."

As the day moved to afternoon and then evening the three continued westward. Finally, they stopped and sat up a campsite.

The fire glowed and crackled. The woman prepared food as the men checked their horses and supplies. None spoke, and when the food was ready, the woman handed a small dish to each man. She then sat down beside the large man and also began to eat.

The large man turned to the woman's brother as they ate. "Do we need to retrieve our guest?"

The young man stopped eating briefly and listened. Then he replied, "No, the guest is approaching slowly in front of us." He then casually returned to his meal.

The large man reached down beside his crossed legs and cocked his musket before he returned to his meal.

While eating, they watched in front of them and across the small campfire. After a few more moments the large man called out, "Please, come to the fire so we can see you. I don't wish to shoot you."

Shortly after this, Onsi crept cautiously into the firelight. He appeared surprised and frightened.

"Sit," was all the large man said to him.

The young man immediately sat down.

To his astonishment, the woman picked up a dish of food and moved over to him. She handed the food to him and then returned to her spot beside the large man. She picked her dish back up and began to eat again.

"Eat," the large man said and returned to his meal.

The Bitter Harvest

All three studied Onsi from across the small fire but said nothing. The young man ate his food quietly and occasionally glanced at the three hosts.

Once all had finished eating, the woman silently collected the dishes. She then pulled a long stem pipe from a leather bag. She filled the pipe with tobacco and lit it with a stick from the fire.

After handing the pipe to the large man, she took a comb from another bag. She moved behind the large man and after untying his long hair began to comb it gently. As she did this, the woman occasionally looked with apparent suspicion at the visitor.

The woman's brother took a piece of wood that he seemed to have saved for after the meal. He examined the wood carefully, but also glanced at Onsi from time to time.

Onsi sat silently as the large man smoked his pipe and studied him.

The woman's brother began to cut the piece of wood with precision and very quickly had ornate designs whittled into it.

Finally, the large man spoke as the fire began to die down.

"I believe you and your people are having trouble. You've searched us out because this trouble is larger than your people can manage. You're hoping to enlist our services, but have little to offer for those services. What we need to know is the manner of trouble you're facing."

The young man was speechless for a moment. The large man continued to stare at him as he pulled another draw from his pipe.

The woman continued to comb his hair, and her brother continued to work on the piece of wood. They all studied the man in apparent anticipation of his answer.

Finally, Onsi spoke with a nervous voice.

"That's very impressive. And I feel sure now that you're the warrior called Orenda."

The large man expelled a stream of smoke from his mouth and replied.

"I am called Orenda, by some. And this is my wife, Nazshoni and her brother Kanuna."

The young man nodded to Nazshoni and Kanuna.

"I'm very happy to meet you. My name is Onsi. And yes, my village is very much in trouble. I have been searching for you for some months now. We feel you may be the only hope we have left."

Onsi paused as if recalling the trouble. Orenda continued to draw smoke from his pipe. Nazshoni combed her husband's hair as she would a daughter. Kanuna focused on the carving in his hands.

Onsi watched them for a few more seconds and then said, "Our village has been ravaged for many months now by a pack of Lofa."

The three hosts froze immediately when Onsi said this. Orenda had been looking into the fire when he froze, and then his eyes drifted slowly up to stare at Onsi.

Nazshoni stopped combing Orenda's hair in mid stroke. She also refocused her eyes from her husband's hair to Onsi.

Kanuna's knife stopped halfway into a cut, and he raised his eyes and also stared at Onsi.

As the silence became very thick, Onsi watched the three. Only the crackling fire and a Whippoorwill in the distance broke the tense atmosphere.

Orenda finally lowered his eyes back to the fire. He pulled another draw from his pipe and as he expelled the smoke, his wife, and brother quietly returned to their activities.

Nazshoni now began tying Orenda's hair back, and Kanuna raised his carving up to get a better look at it in the fading light of the fire.

Onsi waited patiently for some form of reply.

Orenda handed the exhausted pipe to Nazshoni. She carefully cleaned the pipe and placed it in the leather bag. The warrior readjusted himself and Kanuna tossed his carving onto the dying fire, and then he returned his knife and seemed very interested in Orenda's response. Finally, the warrior spoke.

"You can stay here tonight Onsi. We must consider this."

The three then prepared their blankets on the ground and were soon lying down to sleep. Onsi retrieved a blanket from his horse and also lay down to sleep.

Several hours later, Orenda stood up silently and walked into the woods; the moon being his only light. After walking for a bit he stopped and gazed out over a small open area.

He stood in silence for a while. Then, without turning, he spoke, as if talking to the night.

"So, what do you think of this thing my Brother?"

Kanuna silently moved closer to Orenda but remained slightly behind him. He briefly marveled that Orenda always knew of his quiet approach. He replied in a soft voice.

"The Lofa are said to stand seven feet tall. Some tribes call them 'the beasts with big feet.' In the North, they've been called 'Saskewatche.' Most believe an evil Shaman conjured them. They have the stench of a thousand rotting corpses. They're vicious with thick hyde. Their bodies are covered with coarse hair, and their teeth are like those of a wild pig. It's said to be very difficult to kill even one. I had thought the Lofa had been all destroyed years ago."

He paused as if considering his final assessment. Silence briefly overtook the night again. Then he spoke his final thoughts.

"To battle an entire pack of Lofa is almost certain death. But Onsi and his people are right about one thing; you're likely their only hope if there is any."

Again the night became quiet. Kanuna waited for Orenda's response.

Then Orenda said, "And what do you think of this thing my wife?"

Kanuna became surprised as he suddenly realized Nazshoni stood directly across from him, also slightly behind Orenda. He jumped just a little as she turned to him. He could see her smile slightly and felt a bit embarrassed that his sister was able to sneak up on him this way.

She said nothing for a moment. Orenda continued to stare out into the night as his wife considered the situation. Finally, she replied.

"If we should walk past someone that is drowning and they call out for us to help them. And if we also look around to see that we're the only ones that can help them; then we must either risk our lives to do so or forever hear their dying cries in our sleep."

Orenda and Kanuna slowly turned to Nazshoni. They looked at her for several seconds as if very impressed. Orenda then turned back to the open area where the moonlight exposed high grass and several fireflies flashing to each other.

After another moment of silence, Orenda spoke.

"The woman is right. We have only two paths available. And of those two paths, there's only one that we can walk with honor."

Orenda turned and walked back to the camp with Nazshoni and Kanuna following behind.

Onsi woke at dawn. Orenda and the other two sat across from the dead fire; they were staring at him as if waiting for him to wake up.

Sitting up, he tried to think of something to say. "Did I sleep late?"

Rather than answer Onsi's question Orenda began asking one of his own.

"How many Lofa are in this pack?"

Onsi scratched his head as he sleepily considered this.

"We've counted seven, but there seems to be more that stay back in their cave. In the beginning, they would sometimes take our horses too. These were the times we counted at least, seven. But the horses put up a fight and several were kicked very hard. So they stopped taking the horses and only took us. This seems to be an easy thing for them."

Onsi's face dropped a little as if recalling fellow villagers that had become victims. After a few seconds, he continued.

"We've lost seventeen so far, likely more since I've been away. Men, women and children, the Lofa only see us as food. They prey on us when they need meat. I think they may prefer horse meat, but it's easier to kill and drag people back to their cave."

He glanced at the three hosts. His face appeared weary. He continued.

"I believe the chief and elders sent me in search of you because I have no family left. My parents died of a sickness when I was young. I'm not sure that my village thought I could find you, or gain your help if I did. I don't seem to be very skilled at anything."

Orenda, Nazshoni, and Kanuna gave no expression as he spoke, but they listened intently.

Onsi continued, appearing glad to finally tell someone these things.

"Our village is not a large one. We've asked others for help, but they fear the Lofa will turn and prey on their women and children. It's all our men can do to minimize the damage. The ferocity of these beasts can frighten even the bravest of man."

Onsi then glanced up to Orenda. He reacted as if he may have said too much. But neither Orenda nor the others made any expression. They seemed to be taking every word in and building a picture of the Lofa in their minds.

As Onsi noticed this, he also realized how far he'd wandered from Orenda's question. He meekly continued.

"I feel there are at least ten in the pack. They now attack in two's and four's depending on how much food they wish to take. There are always several in the back as reserves, we think."

He then waited for his reply as the sun slowly began to warm the campsite.

Orenda appeared to be studying the ground in front of him. The others turned to him after a long silent pause. He continued to examine the bare dirt. Then he finally spoke.

"Have you and your people talked about moving elsewhere, to get away from the Lofa?"

Onsi replied quickly, "Yes, but no one will leave. The land is ours, and it owns the blood of our ancestors. It's been decided that we will find a way to defeat the Lofa, or we will all die on our homelands fighting them. To move is not an option for us."

The young man looked at the three again. He glanced down and continued.

"I'm a simple man. I don't have skill with words or weapons. But when I saw my friends killed and carried off by those beasts, I decided I must do everything I could to help my village."

Orenda took a deep breath and exhaled slowly.

"We'll assist your people."

Onsi sat up, seeming surprised at the rather quick decision.

"Oh, that's very good to hear. My village will be so happy to have any hope at all. We've almost resigned ourselves to a gradual elimination by the Lofa."

Orenda and the other two nodded with little emotion. Then Nazshoni stood up and began to prepare a small meal as the men packed the horses for travel.

Chapter Two: A Desperate Place

As the four began to traverse the long distance to Onsi's village; he observed the unusual interactions of these three nomads. They spoke very little and yet acted almost as if their minds were united in thought.

The first day Onsi noticed that when Orenda would stop the group for a break, he would cut several straight thin branches from a selected tree. Nazshoni and Kanuna would also cut several long, medium sized branches from a different type of tree. They secured these items to their pack horses and the group then remounted and continued the journey.

Realizing the three were beginning to prepare arrows and weapons for the coming battle, Onsi's heart became heavy. Since the villagers had dispatched him to find Orenda, he had only one thought, to locate the warrior and try to secure his help. Now that this had been accomplished, he began to realize the three may be riding to their death.

That evening around the campfire the four ate before the usual ritual of pipe smoking and Orenda's hair was combed and braided while Kanuna carved a piece of wood. After this, Nazshoni took the thin branches and began stripping the bark from them. Kanuna then examined one of the long tree branches they had cut earlier. After studying if carefully he cut the piece into three smaller sections. He then stripped the bark and laid them out as if to dry.

Onsi sat silently watching the warriors. He wondered about the trail they had traveled so far. Orenda was already a legend throughout the

West. Perhaps not with the white man, but the native tribes had all heard of his skills and the many battles he'd faced. All the tribes respected him.

The next few days they repeated this routine. Then, on the fifth day of their travel, Orenda suddenly turned from the direction they needed to go. He began riding up a small shallow stream with Nazshoni and Kanuna following him; their pack horses in tow.

For an hour or more Orenda moved slowly up this stream. He searched the ground and the woods along the banks of the tributary. It seemed he was looking for a place he'd been before, or maybe he was looking for a place by the terrain, but either way, he eventually moved from the stream; the others followed behind.

After another short period of riding at a slow pace, the group came to an open area with an exposed hillside and rocks laying all along the bottom. Orenda tied his horse to a tree branch and began searching the mass of rocks.

Nazshoni and Kanuna also dismounted and were soon searching the ground as well. Onsi tied his horse, and as he looked over the area, he realized they were searching for stones to fashion into arrowheads and blades for tomahawks.

The three worked silently, and Onsi went to Nazshoni. He spoke softly; "if you show me the ones you prefer, I'll help."

Nazshoni looked through the small batch she'd already accumulated. She picked one out and handed it to Onsi. He nodded and used the example also to collect small flat rocks that were similar in shape and size.

The group worked the rest of the day and only Onsi's words to Nazshoni were uttered. They camped close to the rock quarry.

Onsi awoke during the night to moans from Nazshoni; he dared not move as he didn't wish to interrupt Orenda and his wife. He lay silent and motionless until drifting back to sleep.

The following morning they were up at dawn and soon gathering more of the sharp stones. When Orenda felt there were enough, the four moved back to the stream and by noon was back on the journey towards Onsi's village.

When the small group stopped to camp, they ate, and after Orenda had smoked his pipe and Nazshoni had combed and tied his hair, they would prepare more arrows and tomahawks.

Since Kanuna and Orenda were the only ones that could craft well-balanced arrow and tomahawk heads, Onsi helped Nazshoni assemble the many arrows they would likely need.

Day after day the routine continued. Then the group finally arrived at the river they would follow until reaching the territory of Onsi's tribe.

Several days later, Onsi watched as Orenda stopped. Seeming to spot something he jumped down from his horse and waded into the river. As Onsi came closer, he observed a terrifying sight. A very large and poisonous water snake was moving swiftly towards Orenda. These water snakes were well known to be territorial, and it appeared that Orenda had moved into the water to intentionally provoke the serpent.

Onsi glanced over to Nazshoni and Kanuna who both sat watching Orenda as if he were collecting nuts from under a tree. Neither expressed the slightest concern by this. Onsi then turned back to Orenda who now leaned down as the giant snake swam quickly towards him.

When the serpent was very close to the warrior, Orenda snatched the venomous viper from the water and pulled him out of the river, holding it directly behind its head. The snake writhed about and tried to wrap around Orenda, but he took hold of its lower body and held it with both hands.

Kanuna pulled a large piece of soft leather from the pack horse, and the two put the snake inside and tied it up tightly. Kanuna secured the bag to a pack horse, and they were on the way again.

When they camped that evening, Orenda took a small clay vessel and covered it with a thin piece of leather. Onsi observed with curiosity while preparing some leather strips that would attach the arrowheads to the recently dried shafts.

Orenda then took the bag with the deadly snake and carefully removed it. Onsi felt his skin crawl as the creature moved about in the light of the campfire.

The warrior forced the snake's mouth open, exposing the vipers' long fangs. He pushed the fangs into the thin leather cover of the vessel just as several drops of the lethal venom were developing on the tips. After this, he proceeded to force the liquid from the snake's poison glands.

Though he'd never seen them used before, Onsi knew this must be to produce poison arrows. Again he realized the extent of the deadly struggle ahead for these warriors.

As Orenda held the angry snake to the clay vessel, Onsi rather nervously spoke to ease the tension he felt.

"I hope we can be victorious in the challenge ahead."

Orenda casually glanced up as the viper writhed about to escape and bite its captor. He then looked back at the snake as he considered his reply.

Finally, Orenda spoke in a calm voice.

"For the warrior, victory is rendered with a bitter harvest."

Onsi looked back down to the work in his hands. He thought of what Orenda said. While growing up, he'd always wanted to be a brave warrior. But now, after spending time with perhaps the most courageous warrior of all, he was becoming aware of the harsh realities one such as Orenda faced. During the many days of traveling with the fighters, he seemed to touch the spirit of their world and now knew in his heart that it was a road few could travel.

Every night Orenda would extract poison from the snake and Nazshoni began crafting the arrows which the venom would be used with. She carefully attached small pieces of rabbit hide to the arrows. The sharp point was still exposed, but the little amount of fur past the sharpened point would hold a dose of venom. Onsi tried to help Nazshoni with these, but he wasn't skilled enough and eventually went back to assembling the regular arrows.

For another week, the four traveled along the river. Then they came to the territory of Onsi's tribe; here Orenda released the snake back into the river. The four turned southwest and wearily arrived at the village as dusk was setting in.

Orenda surmised from the huts and layout of the community that there were around three hundred people in this small village. Several scrawny dogs hurried up to the four, barking to alert every one of their arrival. Children ran ahead of them as well, to announce the news of the visitors.

Soon the inhabitants were stepping out of their huts and walking towards the four. The appearance of the community suggested a state of mourning and distress. None of the villagers ventured to greet them. They simply stared and a few nodded slightly to acknowledge them as the procession slowly passed by.

They arrived at a large hut in the central area of the village. A man stepped out and from his elaborate dress; Orenda knew he must be the Chief.

Onsi dismounted as did the others. He stepped up to his leader.

"Chief Hakane, this is the warrior Orenda. He has agreed to help us."

Orenda bowed slightly in respect and the chief then bowed slightly as well to Orenda. He motioned with his hand for Orenda to enter his hut. Onsi led Nazshoni and Kanuna to an empty hut which they would stay in.

Inside Hakane's hut, a light smoke drifted about and intermingled with the smell of the evening meal. His wife moved hastily around the small quarters to prepare food for the special guest.

The two men sat and soon the tribe's shaman arrived and also sat down. The shaman's name was Jacey, and he was around the same age as chief Hakane, who appeared to be fifty-something. Both men had graying hair but expressed confidence and wisdom. The three were soon served a meal, and they quietly ate.

After the meal, Hakane brought out a pipe. He asked Orenda if he would like to smoke and Orenda told him that Nazshoni had his pipe. Hakane then sent his wife to fetch Orenda's pipe; she returned and loaded it with the chief's tobacco.

As the three men smoked and relaxed after the meal, the chief began to speak,

"In the days past we would have had a large feast to honor a warrior such as you. But you've arrived at a heartbroken village that grows closer to death as every day passes."

Jacey nodded and took a long draw from his pipe. Orenda also pulled a draw and listened to the chief carefully. Hakane blew a stream of smoke out and continued.

"We've heard many stories of your honor and bravery. This is why we sent Onsi out to search for you. But in the months since Onsi left on his quest, twenty-two more of our people have fallen prey to the Lofa.

"When the Lofa began to attack and hunt us, we were shocked. They rushed in at night like a fierce wind. They took horses, women, children and men.

"Then after several attacks, we realized the dogs knew when the Lofa approached. They can smell the foul creatures and become very agitated. This was our warning and we felt there may be a chance for defense.

"We sent Onsi out in search of you. We felt you might be our last hope. Then we organized our best and bravest men. When the Lofa approached, we sent them out to meet the beasts and defend the village.

"The men fight bravely and yet they have failed to kill even one of the devils. The sacrifices of our men have kept the Lofa from entering the village again, but every time they go out to defend our people, the Lofa take one or two of them; so our best and bravest have already been lost.

"We've now entered into a state of continual mourning and the feeling that we walk towards death day by day. I'm afraid we have no more happiness to spare for you. We've become hopeless, and even the arrival of a warrior such as you can't bring us out of this dire foreboding."

Orenda pulled another draw of smoke from his pipe and blew it out slowly. He stared into the center of the room, at the ground. The other two men also smoked their pipes and considered the situation. Then Orenda turned to the old Shaman Jacey.

"Is there anything a shaman can tell me about the Lofa? I would like to understand this foe."

Jacey pulled the pipe from his mouth and exhaled a small stream of smoke. He rubbed his chin and then began speaking in a slow but deliberate voice.

"The Lofa is most likely the creation of an evil Shaman. The story I heard years ago from my grandfather was that a shaman began dealing with spirits and magic that no man should be dealing with. He somehow created the first Lofa, perhaps from an evil spirit and a dead body. The Lofa immediately killed its creator and ran into the woods."

Jacey pulled another draw from his pipe. Hakane and Orenda watched him slowly blow it out into the already smoky room. He continued.

"The Lofa became hungry though and returned to the dead shaman. He ate the body, and this perhaps was the source of the Lofa's desire for human flesh. As the days went by, the Lofa observed the women of a nearby village. He captured one and forcefully mated with her. The result was a female Lofa child. He began to prey on villages for food and women to mate with. If the women didn't produce a child, he would eat them."

The shaman paused. He pulled another draw from the pipe. Silence floated in the hazy cabin. Orenda also pulled a draw from his pipe. Then Jacey again continued.

"As time went by, the male Lofa began mating with its daughters. This produced even more deranged and hostile beasts. From all the beasts' offspring, no males were produced.

"Finally, a male was born. This male grew and eventually killed his father and became the pack leader. It mated with the females, and the inbreeding meant many of the offspring died before birth. Those that lived were often deformed and very aggressive. Again, these were all females; only an occasional male is produced to keep the foul creatures in existence. For this reason, the Lofa have not thrived. It's been thought that they had all died, and yet, again and again, one or two stray creatures would turn up and prey on a village.

"This is the first pack I've heard of existing for many years. It's a hard thing that it has taken our village as its feeding ground. I have no magic to fight such a thing. This foe has the strength of several men, the instincts of an animal and the awareness of a man. They're seven to eight feet tall; have the stench of death, teeth of a puma and claws of a bear. The Lofa can move fast in the woods and see well at night. Their hide is covered with coarse hair and is as thick as wild boars. I've not known of a man that has killed a Lofa, though I'm sure it has been done."

The shaman turned his gaze to Orenda, who continued to stare into the middle of the room.

After several moments of silence, Hakane spoke.

"Perhaps it was wrong for us to seek your assistance. You're not of our village or even our tribe. But desperate people will do desperate things."

Orenda slowly turned his gaze to the Chief.

"It was not desperation that brought me to your village. As of yet, I'm not desperate in this struggle. It's also not wrong for you to seek any help possible for your people."

The two elderly men said nothing and all three went back to smoking their pipes. After a while, Orenda asked.

"How do they come and which direction do they come from?"

The chief now spoke as Jacey tapped his exhausted pipe gently and listened.

"They always come from the West, through the ravines. They always come at dusk, and they've always taken at least one or two of our men. They seem content to enter only as far necessary to secure food. They fear fire, but not enough to stop them from attacking."

He then shook his head as if recalling the men taken, and continued in a sad voice, "May the Great Spirit receive our brave warriors with honor.

"These Lofa are much fiercer than any known animal, and though the beasts are not necessarily smart, they do show signs of intelligence. They know when to move to avoid our warrior's arrows. And, if an arrow does hit its mark, it often doesn't penetrate the Lofa's thick hide far enough to do extensive damage.

"If you have a musket, it may help. We don't have such a thing. But you should be aware that the Lofa will adapt to this. We've tried to change our defense plan to surprise them. It works for a short period but they soon alter their moves; we've not been able to do more than hold them off the village."

Orenda continued to stare at the floor in front of him as the chief spoke. He slowly pulled a draw on his pipe only to realize it had gone out. As Hakane finished, Orenda tapped his spent pipe to empty the ashes. He carefully put it back into its leather pouch.

Then he replied.

"Nazshoni, Kanuna and I have faced many challenges, but this appears to be the greatest we'll have faced so far. We'll need the help of every man that can fight. Have them sharpen their knives and prepare arrows. Tomorrow I wish to see the path used by the Lofa."

The two older men nodded in agreement. Then Hakane said.

"We'll do all we can Orenda. But please be aware that these Lofa have ravaged our men. Our bravest warriors have already been taken. Those left are men that shoot a few arrows or throw a spear and run. With some hope, I'm sure they would fight harder, but I can't assure you of much support. We've all been beaten down by this affliction. All of the neighboring villages have avoided us in the hope of not stirring the wrath of the Lofa upon their homes. We've been alone in this fight, and it has us on our knees now."

Orenda nodded, "I understand. Ask your men to do what they can. Any help will be appreciated."

He then motioned as if asking the chief and the shaman for permission to depart from their presence. Both gave their approval as he stood and went outside to Nazshoni and Kanuna.

The following morning Orenda, Nazshoni, and Kanuna stepped outside the log hut. A morning haze intermingled with smoke. The village women busily prepared a meal and brought their guests a portion.

As the three sat and ate, the scrawny dogs came by begging for scraps. Orenda tossed a small piece to one, and then Kanuna tossed a bit to the other. Children moved around the three at a distance as they inspected the visitors.

Onsi approached as they finished their meal.

"Good morning, was your meal satisfactory?"

Orenda stood up, and the other two followed suit.

"Yes, it was fine. Please thank the women that prepared it for us."

Onsi nodded and replied, "Yes I'll do that. Our Chief has asked me to guide you to the path the Lofa use when they attack. When you are ready, I will do that."

"We're all set now," Orenda replied.

"Please follow me then."

Onsi led the way, and as Orenda followed him, Nazshoni, Kanuna, and the scruffy dogs fell in behind them. Then, farther back, several children tagged along at a distance.

The strange procession moved west, out of the village. Soon they came to hills and several long ravines.

"This is where our men take a stand. The Lofa enter the village this way. The pack lives in those mountains. A few of the elders said they had explored the cave now used by the Lofa, but when they were much younger. A bear family lived there before the Lofa came."

Onsi pointed to hills beyond the ravines and a small valley. Even from the distance, Orenda could see the hills were such that housed caves. A warm breeze caressed his face and rustled the leaves in a nearby tree as he studied the area.

"Do the men meet the Lofa here because they can go no farther before the Lofa arrive?"

Onsi replied. "The dogs give us a fair warning. We could go farther than this, but our chief thought this to be the best place for meeting the beasts in battle."

Orenda walked farther into the shallow ravine. The sides sloped, and trees were scattered on both sides. Around fifty yards from the area Hakane designated the battle area, Orenda found some boulders scattered around.

"The Lofa will expect us back there. We'll try to reach this point and surprise them. Several warriors can hide behind these boulders. Others can be among the trees on both sides. I'll place Nazshoni and Kanuna in key positions to inflict the most damage."

He then walked around the new area making plans with Nazshoni and Kanuna. Onsi retrieved several of the higher ranking men, and they also put plans together with Orenda. By mid-day there was a strategy for the defense Orenda would apply.

As the evening moved in, the small group gathered outside the log hut they were occupying. Again the women brought food to them, and they ate in silence as children watched from a distance and the dogs begged for scraps.

After the meal, Nazshoni carefully prepared her husband's pipe and then began to gently comb his hair as he pulled draws and blew them out. Kanuna carved a small ornament, and before they retired to the hut, he gave it to one of the children. The child smiled, and this was the first time Orenda recalled seeing a smile from one of the village children. They slept well that night.

The following morning they again ate a small meal. Men around the camp busily prepared for the coming battle. Around noon, Orenda and Nazshoni went for a walk as Kanuna and Onsi worked on arrows and tomahawks.

The two strolled discretely away from the village. They quietly moved together through a meadow and then along a stream. Neither said anything, but Nazshoni stopped and pulled a wildflower, then smelled it. Orenda simply followed his wife and observed her and the surroundings as they ventured along the bank of the stream.

They arrived at a small waterfall and a pool where the water was deeper than the other areas of the stream. They sat and observed the cascade of water for a while. Then Nazshoni stood up, she slowly took her buckskin dress off and waded into the pool. Orenda picked a piece of wild grass and gently chewed on the stem as he watched her.

She stood naked in the pool and ran her fingers through the water. Then she turned slightly and glanced at her husband. When she saw that he watched her carefully, she smiled coyly and began to pull some of the water up onto her tanned body.

Only the sound of the waterfall and a few birds in the trees could be heard as they spent several intimate hours together.

Later, in the village, Onsi sat a completed arrow beside him as Kanuna worked on another tomahawk. He noticed Orenda and Nazshoni walking towards them. She went inside the log hut as Orenda picked up one of the tomahawks and examined it for balance.

Soon Nazshoni came out with her bow in hand. She handed it to Orenda and he unwound the string and using his strength, he compressed the bow and attached it to the other end. He lifted it up and pulled the string back as if checking its tension, then handed the bow to Nazshoni and she also checked the pressure.

This was the first time Onsi had seen Nazshoni's bow this close. He examined the weapon with interest as he continued to work. It was a beautiful bow and had delicate carvings which gave it feminine beauty. He imagined her brother must have done the elaborate decorations for her.

Chapter Three: Vicious Encounter

An anxious feeling moved through the small village. Another night passed and after the morning meal, Orenda prepared his musket for duty. The children and a few men gathered around to watch curiously as they'd not been this close to such a weapon.

Nazshoni practiced with her bow the day after and again a small audience gathered around the highly skilled bow woman. Her accuracy was remarkable, and Onsi began to feel some hope as arrow after arrow hit its mark.

The next day Onsi approached Orenda and Nazshoni as they examined the arrows that had been treated with the snake venom. As Orenda held them up and moved them side to side, a nasty film could be seen on the points. Onsi's face twisted a little as he imagined being struck with such a lethal projectile.

Orenda commented to Nazshoni as she studied the arrows in her husband's hand.

"These are for your bow only. You should be selective with them. Be sure you have a clear shot and try to strike the largest targets."

Nazshoni simply nodded her head a little and then picked an arrow up to inspect.

That afternoon Orenda looked over spears and an assortment of crude weapons made by the men. He showed several how to hold the shafts and how to jab the long spears into the target. Most of these men were not skilled enough to throw a spear and do significant damage. They were farmers, husbands, and fathers. The majority of the warriors had been taken already.

Onsi considered his abilities as one of the village men jabbed the spear at an imaginary Lofa. He realized he too was sorely deficient in the skills needed to do battle with such beasts. He'd been searching for Orenda while his fellow villagers fought the creatures. Now he wondered if he would drop his spear and run, or if he would stand and fight when the time came. This concerned him, and he paid closer attention to Orenda as the warrior instructed the men. Onsi knew the answer would come soon. The Lofa would be growing hungry by now.

As the day came closer to its end and the sun began to settle on the horizon, a strange calm hovered over the community. The air felt heavy and no breeze disturbed it. The scruffy dogs appeared tense and moved about nervously.

While Orenda, Nazshoni, and Kanuna stood outside the log hut, Jacey approached.

"The Lofa will come this evening. I sense it, as does the dogs. When they begin to whine as if in pain, you should move. The men are preparing now. They will follow you out to the battle area. The Great Spirit will be with you in the struggle tonight."

Orenda said nothing but nodded to the old shaman, who then turned and walked away.

Now he and the other two went inside the hut. Shortly they emerged, and for the first time, Onsi saw the three as pure warriors, ready to do battle.

Kanuna emerged first. His long hair tied back and feathers dangling from the leather hair piece. He wore buckskin breeches and jacket. Over the top was a breastplate made of beads and small bones. Two tomahawks rested in his leather waistband.

As Nazshoni exited the small log hut, Onsi felt excited and slightly jealous of Orenda. She wore a light colored buckskin jacket and breeches. They fit her well and complimented Nazshoni's figure. Her long hair was also tied back, and she wore a leather quiver on her back that was full of the poison snake arrows. Onsi had never seen a woman warrior such as this, much less one prepared for battle. He admired Nazshoni even more at this instant.

When Orenda stepped from the door of the small hut, Onsi felt almost frightened. Though Orenda seldom smiled, he now had a very stoic expression due to the impending battle. He appeared stern and ready for the challenge. He wore no jacket but had an impressive and colorful breastplate. His broad shoulders and muscular arms seemed even more threatening now that the fight was close at hand. He wore buckskin breeches and also had two tomahawks in a leather waistband.

Orenda's tomahawks were obviously of the highest craftsmanship and had iron heads rather than the stone heads that were most prevalent in these areas. In his right arm rested the musket he had acquired at the trade rendezvous. A powder horn and ammunition satchel accompanied the ensemble.

As Onsi studied the three with interest and admiration, the dogs brought him back to the situation at hand. They began to whine and move about as if in pain. Orenda and the others watched curiously as the scruffy canine's tucked tails between their legs and moved about whimpering and expressing fright.

The other men of the village gathered around with their weapons. They watched the dogs and Orenda, who appeared to be studying the group. He then spoke with urgency in his voice.

"Tonight we must be strong, and we must be brave. The enemy approaches, unaware that this night we'll not allow them to have their way. This night, we turn the war around. Are you with me?"

The men moaned in agreement, weakly and without much enthusiasm. Orenda's face became strained now. He shouted, and this time, his voice expressed anger.

"Are you with me?"

The Bitter Harvest

The men became more energized as they shouted out in agreement. As the men raised their spears and bows, Onsi shouted out from a nervous excitement too.

"All right then, let the Lofa's blood run tonight!"

When Orenda said this he turned and took off jogging towards the battle area as the others followed the great warrior.

Onsi rushed to fall in behind Nazshoni and Kanuna. The three seasoned warriors moved like a breeze through the woods and evening light. He struggled to keep pace with them, and the men behind him also began to fall back.

As they approached the area where they would intercept the Lofa, Onsi's spear became heavy, and he labored to bring enough of the warm air into his lungs.

Orenda, Nazshoni, and Kanuna reached the ravine and stood to wait for the village men. Onsi arrived and as he stood trying to catch his breath he became distracted by the three warriors. All three stood calm and not the slightest bit winded from the run. Onsi felt embarrassed and tried to hide the fact he was laboring to breathe.

Soon the village men approached; all were struggling to catch their breath. Orenda looked over the group of around thirty men. He then spoke as several knelt to rest and breathe.

"Don't attack until after I fire the musket. Once I fire, everyone attack. We'll need to strike hard and fast. This is for your village and your families. We must end the Lofa's threat, and that starts here tonight."

He then sent men into the hillsides of the ravine. He positioned Nazshoni behind a large rock that stood beside a tree. Onsi watched nervously as she calmly adjusted her quiver of snake arrows and prepared for the fight.

Orenda then turned to Kanuna, "My brother, that high position over there will be good for your tomahawks. You can send them down from behind the beasts."

Kanuna nodded and took his satchel of weapons up to the area indicated by his brother-in-law. Now, only Onsi stood with his spear in hand. Orenda gazed over the battle preparations and Onsi asked in a withering voice, "Where do you wish for me to be?"

As the light of day faded, the tall warrior turned to Onsi. He studied him for a few seconds and Onsi worried that Orenda would tell him to go back to the village. He felt the great man see the fear in his eyes. He tried to stand tall and brave. Finally, Orenda replied.

"I need you to position yourself over there." He pointed to several trees around twenty yards back to the left and about twenty-five yards directly behind Nazshoni.

Orenda continued in a softer voice.

"Nazshoni has no fear of death. I need you to watch her and help her if needed. We must have her skills with a bow if we're to win this fight. Don't let her know this is your task, though. Do you understand Onsi?"

Onsi felt both proud and terrified that Orenda had placed this responsibility on him. He nodded, "Yes, I understand. I'll watch out for her."

Orenda then began checking his musket as Onsi moved into position. He glanced at Nazshoni in front of him. She pulled a snake arrow from her quiver, and placed it in her bow, but didn't pull it tight yet.

Glancing around at the village men, he could see a few moving about nervously behind trees and brush. Then the smell of the Lofa drifted into the area. Suddenly death seemed to be creeping across the ravine on the slight breeze.

The Bitter Harvest

Onsi placed his hand up to his face to dilute the disgusting smell. One man across the ravine began to vomit. He quickly recovered and as this took place the frightening sounds of the approaching Lofa were heard in the distance.

From in front and perhaps two hundred yards away, a grunting noise mixed with growling entered Onsi's ears. It became apparent that there were a number of the beasts moving towards the group.

The sounds were of a pig mixed with a bear and perhaps a wolf also.

Orenda stared into the growing darkness. The smell of the Lofa was repulsive, but the grunting and growling sounds of the approaching creatures stirred a deep apprehension in the warrior. It was as no sound Orenda had ever heard. As the creatures grew closer, he raised his musket into a ready position.

Onsi turned his attention to Nazshoni again as his heart beat faster and faster. She stood with one foot forward on the large rock. She had an arrow ready in the bow, prepared to pull it taut with pressure and release the projectile into her target. She stared with resolve into the ravine as her enemy approached.

Now Onsi lifted his spear up and turned his attention forward. The faint outlines of the Lofa were seen approaching. They moved about as animals on all fours but occasionally stood up and sniffed the air as a human or bear might. Then the grunting and growling would resume as they again moved forward.

The stench of the foul beasts became much stronger as they slowly crept closer. Onsi wanted to cover his nose. It was the stench of rotting corpses. A sweat bead rolled down the side of his head. He gripped the spear tighter. They were very close now.

Onsi glanced quickly at Orenda who stood like a statue aiming the musket and waiting for his shot. Onsi turned back to the beasts. They were large, perhaps seven feet tall. The Lofa were shaped like a human but had hair all over their bodies, and their arms were slightly longer than human arms. Their faces were not human at all. They appeared as demons would in Onsi's imagination. The face was pulled in slightly and had a black color; they had lower tusks as a wild boar might and small fangs on top as a wolf. Their eyes were dark and vicious.

Now they came into full view. Onsi counted four, and they were well in the target range at this point. With apparent apprehension, the beasts stopped. It seemed they had caught the scent of the humans. Each Lofa stood up on their hind legs and looked around while sniffing the air.

Orenda took aim and the loud 'click, bang' from his musket was heard.

Onsi watched as the musket ball slammed into one of the Lofa, throwing it back into the air and then onto the hard ground.

For a second, the other creatures stood in shock. They looked back at the downed beast and appeared not to understand what had happened or what the loud bang of the musket was. Then, an arrow from Nazshoni's bow penetrated the back of a beast that was examining the one hit by the musket ball.

A growling yell of pain burst from the foul creature's mouth as it reeled from the arrow strike. Immediately another of Nazshoni's arrows struck a different Lofa and this one also screeched in pain.

The Lofa now realized they were under attack and as the village men began shooting their arrows and throwing spears and rocks, the creatures became very aggressive. Everything began to move swiftly as the beasts burst into action.

Onsi's eyes widened as one of the Lofa ran straight towards Orenda, who had sat the musket down and now held a tomahawk in each hand. One of the other beasts moved as a lion, viciously overtaking several of the village men.

The Bitter Harvest

The grip on Onsi's spear tightened, and his blood felt hot. He took several steps back and turned to see the third Lofa charging towards Nazshoni. She stood motionless with the arrow pulled back in her bow. Onsi took off running towards her but knew he wouldn't reach her before the Lofa did.

Just as the beast was springing into the air towards the bow woman, she let the arrow fly and immediately fell to the left. The projectile pierced the beasts' eye and lodged into its skull as it was in mid air.

Onsi stopped as the Lofa tumbled onto the ground twenty feet from him, landing with a grunt against a tree. He then moved towards Nazshoni to fulfill Orenda's request that he watch out for her.

Nazshoni had tumbled away from the Lofa just as she shot the arrow. She rolled several times and was back on her feet, just as a cat might land from a fall. She quickly pulled another arrow from her quiver and began firing at the Lofa which was attacking the men.

The men of the village were trying to keep the creature encircled, and Onsi noticed Nazshoni holding her shots several times to avoid hitting one of the men. The Lofa, in turn, would attack a man and inflict damage, but then the other men would move in with spears. This would cause the beast to release the victim and again take a defensive stance.

As Onsi came closer to the Lofa that Nazshoni had downed with an arrow to the eye, he glanced over to Orenda. This battle was moving at speed Onsi could barely comprehend. His breathing quickened as he stepped up to the small hill and watched Orenda in action.

A few of the men stood with spears and arrows ready, a short distance from Orenda. But the Lofa moved like a large cat, and they couldn't get a shot or spear in without possibly getting Orenda too. The warrior constantly kept his face to the creature as it would attack again and again. He used the tomahawks with skill and often as extensions of his hands and arms. The foul beast would jump towards him and he would extend the tomahawks out, causing the pointed ends to inflict damage on the creature and also keep it from reaching him. He would then roll back, causing the Lofa to miss him. The warrior would quickly be back on his feet and face the beast before it could gain an advantage.

As Onsi reached the small hill and observed the fierce battles around him, the downed Lofa to his side began to stand up. Onsi stared at the creature in disbelief as it slowly rose up onto its feet; Nazshoni's arrow still protruding from its eye. It began to growl and staggered some as if the wound was causing severe pain. Its remaining black eye looked at Onsi with expressed anger and wrath.

He glanced over to Nazshoni and realized she was focused on the other Lofa. He began to tremble as the injured beast started to move towards him.

"Nazshoni, somebody, this one's not dead!" He held his spear pointed at it and glanced over to Nazshoni. She was quickly pulling arrows from her quiver and shooting them, unaware of Onsi's pleas for help.

He backed up as the Lofa began moving to attack. It growled fiercely as dark, almost black blood streamed from the arrow in its eye. As Onsi stepped back, he tripped on something and fell back to the ground. His heart raced as he tried to maneuver the spear in a defensive position.

Just as the injured beast was about to overcome Onsi, something hit it in the front shoulder area. It reared back and screamed out. As it recovered, Onsi realized a tomahawk was buried in its chest and shoulder area. Then, instantly another tomahawk landed in its chest, and as the creature stumbled back, another one landed in its neck area.

The Lofa continued to fall back and landed on the ground with a thud. Onsi turned back to see Kanuna with a tomahawk in his hand, ready to throw if necessary; but this time, the Lofa was dead, and

Kanuna quickly turned back to help his sister battle the beast still attacking the men of the village.

Onsi stood up, trembling from the close call. He turned to Orenda and again witnessed the warrior in his element.

The Lofa appeared to be growing weary as it attacked again and again. Orenda would thwart each advance, and as the beast attempted to recover, the warrior would often inflict blows from the tomahawks. The Lofa screeched out in pain and had cuts on its arms and back from these hits. Orenda would immediately put himself into a defensive position for the next attack. He seemed to be conserving his energy as he fought; slowly wearing the giant beast down.

Several of the village men that had moved away when the Lofa charged were now moving in also to attack the creature that faced Orenda. As it was focused on Orenda, these men would move in and stab it with spears. This caused the beast to turn, and as it moved on the men, Orenda would strike it with a tomahawk.

Onsi turned back to the other remaining Lofa. He moved closer to assist in the battle. This creature had already taken down several men, and their lifeless bodies lay scattered about.

Nazshoni fired another arrow into the Lofa's side. It turned and roared. Onsi was within distance of the bow when the beast charged Nazshoni. She tried to get another arrow out, but the Lofa was too fast. As it closed in on her, she turned the bow as a spear to keep the attacking creature at a distance. The beast took hold of the bow and yanked it side to side, trying to get to Nazshoni. The woman warrior was thrown around as she held the bow tight and tried to keep the Lofa at a distance.

Onsi had never been so frightened in his life, but he ran straight for the creature with his spear, he yelled out and gouged his weapon into the side of the Lofa. It again roared and turned its attention to Onsi, letting the bow drop. Onsi was immediately thrown about as the beast grabbed the spear and hurled him around while struggling to remove it from his flesh.

His act of bravery moved the Lofa from Nazshoni; after the beast had pulled the spear from its side, it let out a tremendous roar and dashed out of the battle area, running over several of the village men on its way out and back in the direction of the caves.

Onsi stood up and glanced over at Nazshoni who was also picking herself up from the ground. She held her side and appeared to be wounded or bruised at the very least.

By this time, darkness was making it difficult to see the struggle between the remaining Lofa and Orenda. Onsi moved cautiously towards the sounds of battle. As he limped forward, lights from torches could be seen moving towards them. His heart lifted as he realized the women and elders of his tribe were moving rapidly towards the battle with lit torches.

As this occurred, he could also see Orenda and the Lofa in an apparent standoff; the beast was obviously wounded and breathing laboriously. Orenda had wounds as well, and his skin glistened from the blood dripping out of his wounds.

Everyone moved slowly towards the two. The Lofa growled aggressively and noticed the torches approaching, turned in an attempt to escape; ran over several men violently knocking them to the ground.

The foul creature ran past Onsi so closely that the stench flowed into his nostrils and again almost caused him to vomit. He staggered backward and watched the wounded beast as it moved past Nazshoni, who also stepped back not to be overrun by the fleeing creature.

As the torches lit the area up and the weary men watched the wounded Lofa run away, Orenda went by Onsi in a flash.

Onsi took another breath, still trying to get the smell out of his senses. He stood in disbelief as the warrior ran in pursuit of the deadly beast. Into the darkness he went. Onsi could barely comprehend anyone pursuing another fight with such a creature. He watched Nazshoni as she attempted to follow her husband, but fell back down, holding her side. The village men stood in the light of the torches, unsure of what to do; seeming to have had their fill of battling the Lofa.

Kanuna took off quickly behind his brother-in-law and was the only one able to follow Orenda into the darkness. As Nazshoni began to crawl in an effort to assist her husband and brother, a terrifying roar could be heard. Then the sounds of a violent struggle erupted. Everyone stood in silence, listening to the fight in the distance.

Suddenly all became quiet. The women and men of the village stood staring into the night. Nazshoni sat motionless, still holding her side and watching for anything to indicate she wasn't a widow.

Then, something or someone approached. Kanuna came into the light of the torches; holding a tomahawk in one hand and appearing dazed. Nazshoni took in a breath and moaned in relief that her brother was alive. But still, she sat motionless, watching for Orenda.

The silence became almost unbearable as all waited. Then Orenda came slowly into the light. He held his two tomahawks and though bloodied and battered it was evident he'd been victorious. Nazshoni finally exhaled in joy at the sight of her husband.

An immediate celebration began as everyone cheered and shouted. All the children and elders of the village began to filter into the battle area and examine the dead beasts. Onsi watched with compassion as some found their fallen family members and quietly mourned over their bodies in the midst of the excitement of finally winning a battle over the Lofa.

Orenda helped Nazshoni up, and Kanuna assisted her on the other side. Onsi obtained a torch and went to them. He thought they would move to the village, but instead, they walked out to the dead Lofa which Orenda had killed before it escaped.

As they came closer to the downed creature, Nazshoni began to walk on her own again. The sounds of the happy villagers became less significant at this place. Onsi became a bit nervous and wondered what the three warriors were doing.

They walked around the dead beast and continued a little farther. Now, in the darkness, other than the light of Onsi's torch, he realized why they came here. Across the valley and in the cave of the Lofa, a tremendous uproar was occurring. Orenda must have heard this after he'd killed the fleeing beast.

The four stood for several moments. There were many Lofa growling and roaring with anger. The one that had escaped must be communicating the fight to the others.

Orenda turned to Nazshoni and Kanuna. Onsi stood back a bit but heard their words clearly.

"We may not survive this fight."

Orendas' face was emotionless as he said this. Nazshoni and Kanuna appeared to give the comment some thought. Then Nazshoni replied with her usual dry tone and lack of expression.

"That's good. I don't wish to mourn either one of you. We'll die together."

Onsi could see a slight surprise on Orendas' face, due to his wife's bluntness. Kanuna also glanced at his sister as if shaken a bit by the hard words.

Orenda considered this for a few seconds and then said with a little more optimism, "We may live, though. We'll make plans for the next battle."

Kanuna quickly picked up on this and also became optimistic, "Yes, we need to make some plans, that'll help."

Nazshoni said nothing and gave no expression to her thoughts. They then moved back to the dead beast that was now being prepared for burning. As villagers piled branches and wood upon the carcasses of the downed Lofa, Orenda, Nazshoni and Kanuna walked to the village to clean themselves up.

All night the villagers celebrated as the foul corpses burned. Onsi watched from a distance but realized the real fight was just beginning. For now, at least, it was good for the people to be happy. They felt there was a chance after all; if only a small one.

Chapter Four: Nazshoni's Story

Onsi woke up the following morning and wandered around the now quiet village. A smoky haze from the still smoldering carcasses drifted over the community area. The smell was extremely rank but far better than the stench of a living Lofa.

Several people moved about, but there was an empty feeling in the air. The dogs even shuffled around sleepily as if the night of excitement had worn them down.

Then Orenda stepped from his hut and Nazshoni followed behind. He said something to her and left. Onsi watched as the warrior moved to Chief Hakane's hut and after a quick knock entered. A short time later Jacey also arrived and entered.

Nazshoni stepped over to a pit and began stirring coals to revive the flames. Onsi walked over and sat down across from her. She appeared tired and still sore from the struggle with the Lofa. As she attempted to revive the fire, Onsi observed the bow woman with interest. He could see she still had pain in her side, yet her face remained stern and without emotion.

An elder woman of the village walked up with some food in a basket just as the fire began to take hold again. Nazshoni sat down all the way, and the woman also sat down.

"Here's something to eat. You must be hungry." The woman smiled at Nazshoni as she handed her a flat loaf and some smoked fish.

Nazshoni thanked her and took the food. The woman then leaned to her other side and handed Onsi a flat loaf and smoked fish as well. He began to eat.

"The men say you fought like a hellion last night." The elderly woman smiled again as she said this to Nazshoni.

The woman warrior stopped chewing briefly and considered the elder woman's words. Then she returned to her food without commenting.

Onsi continued to watch Nazshoni with much interest as he ate his morning meal. Nazshoni was a curiosity to him, and he wanted to know more about her. Not that he had a desire for her, but he'd never met a woman that could fight as she did.

The elderly woman also seemed very interested in Nazshoni and again tried to spark some conversation from her.

"It must be very exciting to be the wife of a great warrior such as Orenda. Did you learn to fight to win his love?"

Nazshoni again slowed down her chewing. But she finished the food in her mouth and appeared to be thinking as she watched the flames. The elderly woman sat with a half smile as she waited for Nazshoni to reply. The fire crackled sharply, and a dog came up to Onsi. He shooed it away and finally Nazshoni began to speak. The tale she told would burn into Onsi's mind, and he would never forget it.

"My tribe was a small one. We lived by a river and between two larger tribes. Life wasn't easy, but we were happy and thought our neighbors were our friends. I was sixteen years old, and Kanuna was fifteen when everything changed.

"One of the larger tribes wanted our hunting and fishing grounds. They made a plan with a small band of rogue savages. This group of murderers came early one morning and took our village by surprise. They killed the men and then the women. My mother told Kanuna and me to hide after my father left to help defend the village. It was the last thing I would hear her say."

As Nazshoni spoke, Onsi saw the half smile fall from the woman's face and slowly a stern face of horror mixed with compassion took its place.

"Once the killers had overrun our men, they began to loot the village and then burn it. They found Kanuna and me hiding under some furs. I thought they would kill us, but instead, they pulled us from our hut and threw us into the middle of the village with some others our age. We huddled together, and many of the young girls wept. We all watched our village burn and tried to spot the bodies of our family members.

"Then, some of the men from the neighboring tribe came. They saw us and said to the leader of the murderers, 'you were supposed to kill everyone. Why did you not kill these too?' The leader replied quickly. 'These people have nothing of value. You either pay us more, or we'll take these and sell as slaves. You said we would get weapons and horses from this village. The horses are broken down, and there are no good weapons here.'

"The traitorous neighbors appeared angry, but they replied to the leader. 'If you do that, then you should take them very far away. We want no word of this to get out. If any of these return and speak of this, we'll hold you accountable.'

"The leader simply smiled and appeared unimpressed. 'If you give us five good horses and ten good muskets we'll kill them all now. Otherwise we're trading them for what you said was here, but isn't.' The traitorous men didn't want to give up good horses and muskets, so they left.

"After this, life became hell day after day as we were forced to move with little food or water. There were twelve of us all tied together and if we had been placed close to a cliff I know we would have certainly rolled off to end our misery."

Nazshoni stopped here and seemed to be reliving the painful moments in her mind. The elderly woman was transfixed on the young bow woman and after a few seconds of thought Nazshoni continued.

"After a week of travel, we grew closer to the slave buyers. One night as we lay together the five men escorting us began to talk. They said the slave buyers would have their way with the fresh young women. Why shouldn't they get us first they reasoned? I watched them in the firelight as they looked at us and spoke of what they would do. I wanted to die right then. If I were to be raped, then I would try to bite the men if possible. I thought of anything I could do to harm them and cause them to kill me.

"Then, as they were about to take us and have their way with us, someone approached from the darkness. The men stood up and told the person to step into the light. This was the first time I saw Orenda. He walked into the camp and said he had seen the fire and wished to do a little trading for some meat.

"He held a musket in one hand and his horse's reins in the other. It was a fine horse, and our captors immediately began to eye the animal and the musket with desire. Orenda seemed unaware of this and also unaware of us.

"Sit down friend; they told Orenda. 'We'll talk about trading.' I watched this and thought, oh poor man, they'll soon kill you and take everything. Orenda sat down and began to talk with them. Then he looked over at us. 'What do you have there?' He asked. 'Oh, we're going to trade those for some muskets and horses,' they replied.

"Orenda looked us over again with interest, 'Well, I might trade this musket for a few if you would like.' Now I became even angrier. I hoped something might happen with the arrival of this man, but now he would try to trade for us and then die as well. Our captors replied, 'Oh yes, that'll be good as it'll be less trouble for us.'

"I glanced into Orenda's eyes as he looked us over once more. I saw something, but I wasn't sure what it was. 'How about the girl there and the young man beside her,' he pointed to Kanuna and I. 'Yes that will be good' the men said, but I knew they only wanted to get the musket and then they would kill him.

"So, Orenda handed one of them the musket. *Now he will die,* I thought. The man turned the musket towards Orenda and pulled the hammer back. 'What's this?' Orenda said. 'We agreed to trade, and you said it was fair. Are you betraying me?' The men laughed. 'You fool; we'll still sell those to the slavers and have your horse and musket as well.' Orenda backed up several feet, holding his arms up. The man pulled the trigger, and the musket fired. Orenda fell back into the bushes. But did he fall back from the musket ball? I realized he fell back and rolled. It was hard to tell as smoke from the musket was everywhere.

"The man that held the musket and examined it strangely. 'There was no ball in it' he said, 'only powder.' They instantly looked to the bushes that Orenda had fallen into. For a second, I saw fear on the men's faces. But at this instant, two knives flew from the bushes and had landed in the chests of two of them. Then a third knife came flying out before they could react and another man looked down at the blade in his heart before falling to the ground dead.

"Two men were left now and they turned to run. A tomahawk landed on the back of one before he reached the edge of the campsite. As the other ran, Orenda stepped from the bushes with another tomahawk in his hand. He stood and took aim. The tomahawk flew through the air, and the sound of it landing on the fleeing man's back could be heard."

Nazshoni stared into the fire as if it helped her remember. The crackling blaze and a dog barking in the distance were the only sounds for a brief moment. Then she continued.

"Orenda untied us. We told him of our plight. He fed us and gave us water. The next day he talked of a village he would take us to. He said the people were kind, and he was certain they would adopt us into their community. But as we made our way there, I decided that I would not leave this man. I told my brother, and he said, 'I'll not leave you then; you're the only family I have now.'

"After a long journey we came to the village, and as he had said, they were kind and understanding. We ate and were invited into their community. But I watched Orenda. He was in his early twenties at that time. I know that I had fell in love with him, but I refused to believe it. I told myself that if I could only stay close to him, then I would be content.

"A few days passed and he left the village. Kanuna and I followed behind. He traveled slow and soon realized someone followed him. He caught us and sat us down. 'Why are you following me,' he asked. I replied, 'we belong to you. You traded for us, did you forget this?'

"Orenda stared at me, but his eyes held compassion. 'You're free now. You can do what you want. I don't wish to own you,' he said.

"I thought about this and then asked him, 'Are we truly free? Can we do as we wish now? 'Yes, certainly,' he replied. I said, 'then we wish to stay with you.'

"He smiled at this answer but became serious again. 'You don't wish to stay with someone such as me; you'll not live to see gray hairs on your head if you stayed with me.'

"I quickly replied, we wouldn't have lived to see those gray hairs if you'd not saved us from the slavers, so it matters little to us."

Onsi noticed the sun creeping into the village now and burning off the smoky haze. People began to move about, and a few children chased one of the scrawny dogs around.

Nazshoni continued.

"Orenda considered my words. He studied the two of us. Finally, he said, 'You can travel with me a short distance. But you'll see the life I live and change your minds. Death sleeps beside me and often waits around the bends for an ambush. I live day to day not knowing what battle may lie ahead. The Great Spirit made me what I am, and I don't complain. But it's not the life I would choose if I had a choice such as you do.'

"We didn't choose to have our family murdered and our home destroyed, I replied. The Great Spirit chose to put us with you, so it would be good for you to teach us to fight and we'll be your allies rather than burdens.

"Again I saw a slight smile on his face, and I knew there was hope. As the days passed, he became fond of us and did begin to teach us. We soon realized that Orenda is a warrior who fights for honor and goodness. When you fight for such things, you must be very strong, because evil always outnumbers such warriors.

"As I grew older and we traveled, I noticed that Orenda was falling in love with me and I was very happy. When I was eighteen, we were married. Two days after our marriage we were fighting the renegade War Chief 'Blood Hawk.' Death has been our constant companion, and I know someday we'll die in battle together. But I would have it no other way. Orenda was born to be a warrior and to love him and live with him means also to die with him. He fights with honor, and so I fight with honor too, and I will die with honor beside him."

Nazshoni stopped here and still gazing into the fire picked up a stick and stirred the coals again. Embers danced up into the air. A dog continued to bark at the children as if to chastise them for chasing him about. Onsi glanced at the elderly woman and noticed several tears rolling slowly down her cheeks. He also wanted to cry but didn't.

The woman warrior began to eat again, and Onsi realized he'd held his food the entire time she spoke. He began to eat as well. Then he

The Bitter Harvest

glanced back to the chiefs' hut and wondered what the conversation was inside.

In the dimly lit structure, Orenda sat across from Chief Hakane and the Shaman Jacey. Smoke from their pipes danced all around as if intermingled with the men's thoughts.

"We'll need a plan and more men if we're to have any hope against the next attack. There are at least six or seven more Lofa, and they won't be caught off guard again."

After Orenda said this, the men again pulled draws from their pipes and considered the situation. Then Hakane spoke.

"I'll send riders to our neighboring villages. They've been afraid to become involved as we've had no victories against the Lofa. After our success last night they may send help. I suspect they're aware that once the Lofa get through us, one of their villages will be next. It's the only thing I know to do. We have very few men left, and we lost three more of what we had last night."

Orenda turned to Jacey, "How long before the Lofa come again?"

The shaman considered this and after slowly expelling a stream of smoke he replied. "A day or two maybe; they'll likely hunt a few small animals to ease their hunger, but after they get over the shock of the lost battle, they'll be back. When they return, they'll be hungry and extremely hostile. I would say we need to act without haste."

Orenda also expelled a stream of smoke out. "They'll be expecting a trap... but perhaps not two."

Hakane and Jacey slowly turned and looked at him. They smiled slightly as they both pulled draws from their pipes. Then Hakane nodded, and Jacey did as well. Orenda also grinned slyly as they all considered the next step.

While the day moved closer to noon, an excited but stressed feeling came over the small village. Riders left quickly on their way to neighboring communities. Orenda moved about with Hakane and Jacey as they prepared for the certain attack.

Onsi followed behind the three leaders as they searched the areas around the previous night's battle.

"Here, they'll need to come through here unless they go through the thick brush and around the ridge. Will they do something such as that?" Orenda glanced back to Jacey as the old shaman leaned on his staff.

"I don't think they'll travel the long way around to attack. You must remember these Lofa are more animal than man. They're inbred and twisted by the evil spirit inside. I don't think they have the ability to make a lengthy or detailed plan. However, in place of civilized thought, they have keen senses and a degree of awareness that other beasts don't have. They will likely anticipate another trap and be wary. But I suspect they'll come at us by the easiest path."

Then Chief Hakane added, "They'll come fast and with much violence, though. We must be prepared for that."

Orenda considered this a few seconds before replying. "We'll set the first attack for here. As they come through this way, we can move back across this shallow area and lead the beasts to the open field there. That is where the real fight takes place."

Onsi looked back to where Orenda pointed. It was an open area that had plenty of room for a battle in the middle. It might work Onsi thought. His hopes increased.

Back towards the now bustling village, they went with a purpose in their steps. Nazshoni had the women and older children busy assembling more arrows. Kanuna worked with the men preparing spears and tomahawks. The scrawny dogs moved about nervously, and everyone sensed the urgency of the situation.

Orenda gazed out over the activity. Jacey then spoke.

"We'll have many arrows, but few men to send them in flight."

"Will others come?" Orenda asked.

Hakane thought and then spoke with little enthusiasm. "Your name alone carries weight. I believe some warriors will come if only to say they fought beside Orenda. But beyond that, it's hard to say. The Lofa is thought of as a scourge or malady. Although these villages know their family and community may be next in line unless they're stopped here, they also don't wish to do anything that may provoke the Lofa into choosing their people to prey on over others. We'll have to wait and see I suppose."

Soon there were men and women working around the area Orenda chose to fight in. Everyone struggled to make preparations before nightfall but too soon the sun began to set.

"There's not enough time," Nazshoni said as she walked beside her husband. "We won't be ready."

Orenda took a deep breath and looked over the hasty preparations. "We'll just have to do the best we can. They can work no faster, and most are already exhausted. If they're pushed any harder, they'll not be able to fight."

She glanced at him and then they moved on towards the village to prepare themselves.

As they walked into the community, riders on horseback moved into the area. Dogs barked and followed the strangers into the village center. There were eleven men, and these were obviously fit young warriors. They carried bow and arrows along with other weapons. Immediately an excitement stirred.

The leader stepped down from his mount in front of Orenda and Nazshoni. He was a large man, similar in size and stature to Orenda, but several years younger. He appeared proud and brave.

"You are Orenda, the warrior that defeated Blood Hawk?" He asked after approaching.

"That's what some call me. But I didn't defeat Blood Hawk alone; I had help."

The warrior appeared impressed with Orendas' answer.

"Yes, but it's said you're the one that removed his head in battle. Many tribes that were victimized by Blood Hawk and his men would have liked for his fingers to have been removed one by one, as he watched. But nevertheless, we were all glad to hear of his demise."

Orenda expressed approval of this reply. The warrior continued.

"I'm Lonato; we've come to fight the Lofa with you. I wish there were more, but few feel there's a chance of surviving a battle with these unclean devils."

Orenda nodded and replied.

"You're enough to raise our hopes at the very least Lonato. And this means more right now than you may realize."

Lonato also nodded as his fellow warriors dismounted.

The evening was rapidly approaching, and tension grasped the air as last minute preparations was made.

The women moved into the huts with children, and the group of fighters followed Orenda to the battle area.

Lonato and the warriors with him grimaced and stared with a curious interest at the still smoldering Lofa carcasses.

Orenda directed everyone to their positions as the last light gave way to darkness.

On the line of the ridge and across from the Lofa cave, Orenda sat quietly with Nazshoni. As darkness settled in, the Lofa could be heard. They growled and roared. There seemed to be some fighting as well. The valley echoed with the terrifying sounds. Nazshoni stared into the darkness. Orenda placed his arm around her. She was surprised by this at first but then moved into his embrace. Time moved slowly as they waited.

Throughout the night the Lofa pack moved around the cave. They would move outside, and Orenda would sit up. Nazshoni would also stir from an uneasy sleep, and both would become ready. Then the Lofa would move back into the cave with roars and unearthly growls. More infighting might occur, along with screeches of pain. Then all would settle down, and Orenda would doze briefly.

Finally, as daylight began to break over the horizon, all became quiet in the Lofa cave. Orenda stood up and stretched. He glanced down at Nazshoni.

"It seems we have another day to ready ourselves."

She nodded in agreement, and they moved towards the others.

In the area prepared for the battle, Lonato, Onsi, and the others emerged from their hiding spots as Orenda and Nazshoni arrived. Lonato spoke to Orenda as soon as he came close.

"We could hear the black devils from here. How many do you suppose there are?"

"Seven to ten I think," Orenda replied and then continued. "But we have a better chance now. We can complete the traps today. It sounded as if they wanted to attack several times last night but backed out. I believe tonight their hunger will prevail. But we'll be better prepared due to their reluctance."

Lonato agreed, and after a meal, the men and women went to work completing the ambush area.

Chapter Five: Trapping Devils

That afternoon Orenda went to talk with Hakane and Jacey. Again the three sat in the smoke filled room. Hakane's wife brought in some food, and they ate. Then the three men filled their pipes and smoked as they contemplated the situation. Finally, Orenda began to speak.

"The Lofa's are very agitated. We may have only one chance to win this fight."

Hakane nodded and replied. "Four more warriors came today from neighboring villages. The word of our victory against the Lofa is getting out. But still, few are ready to enter the battle."

Jacey now joined in the conversation as he expelled a draw from his pipe.

"Perhaps an encouraging talk with the men that we do have would help. Strong words can temper a warriors' heart before a battle."

When Jacey said this, Chief Hakane looked at Orenda. The warrior turned his attention to the chief. Both seemed to know what the other one thought. Finally, Hakane spoke.

"You should talk to them Orenda. They would follow you into the Lofa's lair if you asked them to. I'm old, and can no longer fight, or I fear, inspire the men."

Orenda replied immediately. "I respectfully believe you should talk to them not me. You're their Chief; their neighbor and friend. You're their leader. You've been in this battle with them from the beginning, and you should remain in it with them. You're still a brave warrior, and they'll listen to the words of their chief."

The Bitter Harvest

Hakane gazed through the smoke as Orenda now pulled another draw from his pipe. He considered the warriors' words. Jacey watched the two with interest. Then Hakane replied.

"No matter what happens at the end of this path my friend, I am proud to have met you. You truly are a warrior with honor. You have the spirit of a puma and the vision of an eagle. Your words are true. I'll speak with the men."

Jacey smiled. Orenda nodded. They finished their pipes and considered the events to come.

Later, as Orenda walked around the preparations inspecting them, Chief Hakane came to the site. The sun was now giving its last few hours of light as Jacey called the men to gather around their Chief and neighbor.

Hakane began to speak with a confident voice, "Friends and neighbors, Lonato, and those who've come to help in our time of need." He paused and gazed at the men. "We're here to put an end to this suffering. Ours and those black heart devils that belong in the fires of the earth."

Hakane now began to move about slowly, using his staff. He spoke to the men and looked into their eyes one by one.

"We will destroy them and avenge our fallen. We are strong and fierce. We've killed some of these demons, and we'll not stop until this grim task is over, and our homes and families are safe once again. We'll become entangled with vile beasts tonight and blood will flow, but when this foul work is done, we'll be the ones standing, not them."

Now the men began to whoop and yell in agreement as excitement stirred. Orenda glanced over to Jacey, and he smiled. Hakane raised his staff and finished with a loud voice.

"This is our hunting grounds, not theirs. We're going to send those devils back to the pits they came from!"

Now the men raised their weapons and shouted out. They danced around, and the energy was felt throughout the group.

As the men calmed some and began to take their positions, Kanuna came to the area carrying Orenda's musket.

Nazshoni also arrived with her bow and arrows. The three seasoned warriors expressed confidence and calm. Onsi felt a rush of pride as he watched them from a distance. If he died tonight, he would know he fought with honor beside these brave warriors. He moved to his position as the day was losing its struggle with the night.

Again the area became quiet as the wait began. This time, Orenda remained in the ravine leading to the battle position. This would be the starting point. On his left and right, in the brush, men with spears waited. Onsi was one of these men on the left of Orenda.

Soon the Lofa could be heard across the valley. Again they roared and growled. They ventured out from the cave and then back in. More fighting occurred inside the cave. Then they moved outside. This time, they didn't go back in. The Lofa were headed towards the village. Orenda cocked his musket and stared into the night.

The air became thick as the creatures made their way across the valley. Then, even the Lofa became quiet. Onsi began to sweat as his ears strained to hear the beasts.

After what felt to be a long stressful moment, he could hear something moving towards them. He could barely make out two, and then three and four; finally, two more moved cautiously into the ravine.

The dark beasts brought the horrendous smell with them, and Onsi could feel his stomach turn from the stench. They crawled about sniffing the air and searching the area with their black eyes.

As the six Lofa crept cautiously past Onsi and the other men that were hiding, a 'click' sound was heard. A flash of light and a loud bang rang out from Orenda's musket. Onsi heard the ball hit one of the Lofa, but the flash of the powder had caused his eyes to lose sight briefly.

With this shot, the battle began. The men came out of hiding throwing spears. The Lofa began to attack, and several men were immediately slaughtered. Onsi could feel his heart pounding rapidly in his chest.

With spears and tomahawks, the men fought, but some moved with purpose back towards the large open area. The Lofa pursued the men, and again several unfortunate fighters were killed violently.

Behind the Lofa, Lonato and his men began lighting torches. As the Lofa came into the battle area, the men moved to the sides and Nazshoni along with ten other men that were good with the bow and arrow fired shots into the beasts.

Roars and growls rang out as the Lofa were hit again and again. As Lonato and his men moved towards the battlefield, the Lofa screeched out in fear of the light.

Onsi quickly moved back to the brush which had been set aside. The men threw the brush behind the creatures and Lonato, and his men set it ablaze. The Lofa were trapped.

Nazshoni and Kanuna rapidly fired arrows and tomahawks at the creatures.

The Lofa now began to fight with a renewed fury. They moved like lions and killed any man within their grasp.

Orenda entered the fight with a tomahawk in each hand. As the fires lit up the killing zone, Onsi watched the warrior land a blow on the arm of a Lofa. It howled out in pain and turned on him.

As the beast began to charge Orenda, one of Nazshoni's arrows landed on its side. Again it howled, and with this distraction, Orenda moved on the creature with both tomahawks. Two blows into the beast in rapid succession. The Lofa staggered back.

Onsi tried to grasp the terrifying situation. Lonato and others now circled the battle area with torches. The remaining Lofa ran about wildly, attacking the men but seeming to fear the fires more than anything else.

To avoid being caught from behind, Onsi moved towards one of the Lofa that had now been cornered by the men. He glanced back nervously and then moved with his spear to the raging beast.

The creature was growling and foaming at the mouth as Onsi came to assist the others. Fear gripped him as he jabbed the creature. It snarled and lashed out at the men.

Onsi fell back to the ground and saw the Lofa grab one of the men from his village. The beast swung the screaming man around as if he were a small branch and then the man went flying over Onsi and landed hard about twenty feet away from him.

Trying desperately to find the courage to stand back up he glanced over to Orenda. The warrior had inflicted heavy damage on the Lofa, and as Onsi watched, he moved in for the kill.

The Lofa staggered and once again tried to attack Orenda. The warrior stepped aside and buried the tomahawk in his right hand into the beasts' chest. Then the tomahawk in his left hand immediately swung around and landed with a thud on the back of the creatures head. It stood for a second and Orenda pulled his weapon from its chest. Then the Lofa fell to the ground dead.

Onsi scrambled to stand up. He was terrified that Orenda might spot him lying on the ground.

As he gained his footing, the Lofa he had jabbed with his spear broke from the circle of men and ran straight over him. He landed hard back on the ground and had difficulty catching his breath.

Nazshoni came and stood close to him as he lay helpless. She pulled an arrow from her quiver, and her aim followed the rampaging beast.

Onsi held his chest in pain but turned to view the creature. It ran towards the fires and then turned. Nazshoni let her arrow fly, and it landed in the Lofa's chest. It stumbled back but spotted Nazshoni as she quickly pulled another arrow and placed it in her bow.

The beast began to charge. She let the arrow fly. It landed in the Lofa's neck, but it kept charging. Nazshoni stood firm by Onsi and pulled another arrow from the quiver. She wouldn't have enough time. The Lofa was to close. Onsi braced for the impact.

Suddenly Orenda came from the side and leaped onto the creature before it reached Nazshoni and Onsi. The two rolled away from the bow woman who had never flinched. She now had the arrow in her bow and anxiously searched for an opportunity to send it into the beast as it and Orenda tumbled to a hard stop. Both immediately stood and took a fighting position.

Nazshoni stepped away from Onsi and moved towards Orenda and the Lofa, which were squaring off. Orenda had his back to Nazshoni, and she tried to move at an angle to hit the Lofa but not Orenda.

Onsi stood up and attempted to grasp his spear. Holding it as a staff, he began to move towards the fight.

To his left, Kanuna and several others were struggling with another of the foul devils. One of Kanuna's tomahawks could be clearly seen embedded in this Lofa's back. Even so, it had several dead men around it and continued to fight fiercely.

Lonato and his men encircled the other two beasts. Some of the warriors that came late were also in the battle with these two.

As Onsi came closer to Nazshoni, she let the arrow fly, and it hit its mark in the Lofa's throat. It growled out and took the arrow to pull it out. But now Orenda moved up quickly and landed a tomahawk blow in the neck of the beast and almost removed its head. The Lofa fell dead and immediately Orenda and Nazshoni moved to assist Kanuna.

Onsi turned as the two moved passed him. He limped towards the fight as the Lofa almost caught Kanuna. While the young warrior dodged the grasp of the creature, he swung his tomahawk and almost removed the beast's claw. Enraged by this painful blow, the Lofa grabbed a village man as he attacked with a spear and swung him violently across the battlefield. As it did so, Kanuna landed a tomahawk on the back of this beast's skull. Still, it attempted to fight. Kanuna and the other men moved in quickly to kill the creature.

Nazshoni had placed another arrow in her bow, attempting to get a clear view of the beast. When she couldn't get a good shot, she turned to the two Lofa that Lonato and his warriors were fighting. Soon she let the arrow fly, and it hit one of the beasts in its chest. She quickly pulled the last snake arrow from her quiver and let it fly.

The Lofa that Nazshoni hit with this arrow staggered about and lashed out at the warriors. Lonato saw an opportunity now and taking aim let lose his spear. The weapon hit its mark, and the beast fell to the ground. The remaining Lofa, however, struck one of Lonato's men and almost removed his head. The warrior was dead before hitting the hard earth.

After this, the Lofa broke lose from the encirclement and ran away from the fires. It was headed towards the village.

As it went by Orenda, he moved to intercept it and landed a blow from his tomahawk into the beast's leg.

The creature roared out and tumbled to the ground. It finally slid to a stop and attempted to stand back up. Orenda raced up to the creature. It foamed at the mouth and lashed out at him, but he waited and at the right second moved in and impaled his tomahawk into the beasts' skull.

Everything became strangely quiet now. Onsi stood in awe that he was still alive. Orenda removed the bloody weapon from the dead creature. Nazshoni looked to her little brother who now examined one of the dead Lofa.

As some assisted the wounded, others stared at the lifeless beasts.

Orenda came closer to Onsi who had yet to find the strength to move. The warrior had a concerned expression.

"We won," Onsi said weakly. But Orenda still seemed unsatisfied.

"There's something wrong here," the warrior replied.

"What, what's wrong? We won, right?" Onsi then again looked over the battle ground. He couldn't see what Orenda spoke of. The Lofa were dead.

Orenda continued to examine the dead beasts. Finally, he replied. "These are all females. There's always a male in the pack."

Onsi now began to look around. He remained in the same spot but gazed about trying to spot a male. Orenda walked back to the last creature killed and inspected it again.

Suddenly, with a burst of flames and embers, a huge beast came through the burning brush. Onsi nearly fell over from shock. It was undoubtedly the male.

Kanuna was almost directly beside the beasts' entry point and as he tried to move away he fell. The massive creature grabbed him by the leg and threw him across the battle area as if he were a twig.

Nazshoni screamed in terror when she saw this and reached back to grab an arrow. There were no more in her quiver. She pulled the knife from her leg strap and immediately took off running.

Onsi wanted to move. He knew she intended to attack the beast. He wanted to help her, but he was frozen. She ran towards the front of the creature screaming "I'll kill you, I'll kill you!"

As everyone stood in shock, a yell as never heard before came from behind Onsi. The beast looked back. Nazshoni stopped and looked back; as did Onsi.

Orenda stood beside a dead Lofa. He then viciously buried a tomahawk into the dead creatures' skull. He pulled it out and held it in the air, yelling out again in a victorious but angry way that the huge Lofa must have understood. It stood up on it legs now and was, at least, eight feet tall. It growled, and saliva dripped from its massive mouth.

Nazshoni now ran over to Kanuna. She knelt down beside her brother holding the small knife out in a protective manner. She wept, and Onsi stepped back in a daze, feeling all was falling apart.

Before anyone could do anything other than stare in shock, Orenda took off running towards the huge male. Seeing this, it knelt down as if to take the Warriors' charge head on. Onsi couldn't believe it. This massive male Lofa would surely tear the warrior apart.

Unexpectedly, Orenda stopped in mid stride and let one of his tomahawks fly. With the momentum gained from the warrior's short sprint, the weapon whizzed past Onsi. The huge male Lofa barely saw this in time and moved just before the projectile landed on its head.

But directly behind the male beast and unseen in the darkness was another female. When the male quickly moved, the tomahawk landed square in this females' forehead. It grunted and then slowly fell to the ground dead.

Orenda again yelled out in anger. Onsi looked at the huge male and saw fear in its black eyes. It was the most incredible thing he'd ever witnessed. The male stood up and howled out in anger. But it then turned and left the area hastily.

With the male gone, Orenda ran to Kanuna and Nazshoni; she was weeping now and holding Kanuna in her arms. He was either dead or unconscious. Orenda picked Kanuna up and ran towards the village.

Onsi shook his head in disbelief. What had happened? He thought they had won. He felt as if he would fall, but instead simply sat down on the ground and watched Nazshoni following behind Orenda. The other men appeared to be in shock as well.

All night long men kept the fires burning; hoping to keep the male Lofa away. Large blazes also burned in the village as the women helped the wounded. Onsi starred at Jacey's door and wondered how Kanuna was. Every so often a woman would come out and get water or something else and take it back in quickly.

Onsi finally sat down and soon fell asleep from exhaustion. In his dream, the male Lofa appeared; his face violent and gruesome. On and off throughout the night, the beast tormented Onsi with nightmares.

Chapter Six: Blood Song

Onsi awoke to find the dawn slowly breaking over the tree tops. The two scrawny dogs barked in the distance, somewhere around the battlefield. A smoky haze from the fires once again lay over the now calm village. He stood up and stretched his sore body. Then he walked to Jacey's hut, where Kanuna had been taken.

A dark and foreboding scene presented itself to the young man as he gently opened the door. The dim morning light streamed in to reveal Kanuna lying on a bed. His leg was positioned to stay in place by two straight sticks, indicating it was broken. Wounds on his body had been tended and though no longer bleeding, revealed the damage done by the brief encounter with the male Lofa.

Nazshoni sat beside her brother and had her head down in one hand. She appeared exhausted when she glanced up at Onsi. Her eyes were still swollen from the many tears she must have shed through the night.

In a dark corner stood Orenda, his face strained with concern.

Onsi quietly closed the door behind him and stood motionless for a few seconds. Nazshoni stood up and walked over to him. She gently touched his arm and attempted a smile, and then she stepped behind him and went outside.

Walking over to Kanuna's bedside he sat on a small stool and looked at the injured warrior. Kanuna opened his eyes very slightly. He gazed up at Onsi and smiled just a little. Onsi couldn't help but smile back due to Kanuna's bravery.

"You'll be all right my friend. Just rest and get better." Onsi then patted Kanuna's arm. He glanced back at Orenda, and the warrior nodded to him as if glad for Onsi's comforting words to his brother-in-law.

Kanuna closed his eyes again, seeming to drift back to sleep.

Orenda walked over to Onsi.

"Can you stay with him for a while?"

Onsi nodded that he would.

"I'll have some food brought in for you and Kanuna, in case he wakes up and can eat anything."

Again Onsi nodded. Orenda patted him on the shoulder and left.

Later that morning Orenda stepped into Chief Hakane's hut. The chief and Jacey both sat as if waiting for him. Orenda sat down, and Hakane's wife brought several plates of food for the men. They ate quietly and afterward lit up their pipes and smoked. Again Orenda started the conversation.

"It's become personal now, between the male and I. He knows I've brought much destruction to his pack. He wants me, and I want him. One of us must die."

The two elder men looked at Orenda. They considered his words as they smoked. Then Hakane spoke.

"Is he the last?"

"I'm not sure," Orenda replied. "The female I killed, which stood behind the male, appeared to be the dominant female. She was positioned directly behind the male as if this were her rightful place. But I'm not certain if she was the last female or not."

He paused and pulled another draw from his pipe, then continued.

"The male will come for me. But how and when is the question. I believe that I placed some fear in his heart. But this will also make him more cautious. The problem now is determining what his next move will be."

Oliver Phipps

Orenda looked at Jacey, and the shaman considered it. Then he replied in a voice of resolve.

"I think the male will wait for every advantage to be in place. He may not be as concerned about survival now, but rather wants to kill you, regardless of anything else. These beasts have an evil and black heart. Anger and revenge will be burning inside him. But the side of him that has a man's thoughts will consider his action before making a move. When he does move, though, you should expect a fierce battle. I feel certain that this male will go through anything or anyone to kill you."

The three sat in silence again. Orenda finished his pipe and tapped the ashes into the small fire.

"Then it's for certain that I must kill him first."

The warrior stood up and left.

As he exited Hakane's hut, the foul smell of the burning Lofa turned his nose. In the area of the battle, smoke rose as the villagers burned the corpses. Even scorched with a blazing fire, the Lofa smelled so foul it would turn a strong man's stomach. He moved on to Jacey's hut to check on Kanuna.

Upon entering, he could see Nazshoni trying to feed her injured brother some broth. Kanuna appeared barely awake and only took a very small sip. Nazshoni glanced up to her husband. She sat the small bowl down and came to him.

"The stench from those foul creatures' carcasses would keep a healthy person from eating."

Orenda nodded, "Yes, but the sooner there's nothing left of them, the sooner the air will grow fresh again."

He then went and sat beside Kanuna.

"How are you, brother?"

Kanuna opened his eyes slightly. He tried to nod his head as if he would be all right. He coughed and grimaced from pain.

The Bitter Harvest

"Hmm, you'll be all right then. It'll take more than a few Lofa to kill you. You should eat, though." Orenda then leaned down to him and whispered. "I'll have your sister cover your nose for you while you eat. We'll get a good laugh about it later."

Kanuna opened his eyes slightly and smiled. Orenda smiled also. He then patted Kanuna's arm and stood up.

"Did he speak?" Nazshoni asked with urgency.

"Well, there was something mentioned about you covering his nose while he eats. The smell of the dead Lofa is just too much."

"Oh... all right, I'll do that." She then went over and attempted to cover his nose with one hand; she fumbled with the bowl in the other; trying to feed her brother.

Kanuna opened his eyes slightly and glanced up at her and then over to Orenda. He again smiled, and Orenda also chuckled at the humorous sight of his warrior wife's difficulty with a bowl of broth.

Once the warrior had stepped back outside, Lonato approached him.

"How's your brother-in-law?"

"We don't know yet. He has a strong spirit, though. I'm sure he'll fight and survive, if at all possible."

Lonato considered this. He then replied. "He'll be sorely missed when the male returns. We lost four men from our village. Seven men altogether and six wounded, counting Kanuna."

Orenda began to walk through the hazy village and Lonato followed by his side.

"This male, I suspect he wants me more than anything else. I believe he understands clearly that I came to destroy the pack. Although he retreated last night, he'll return soon for revenge. I think we may be able to use this as an advantage."

Lonato looked at Orenda with a confused expression and then asked.

"Are you suggesting we use you for bait?"

Orenda stopped and thought about this. His mouth twisted slightly as he exhaled.

"Perhaps, if that's what we must do; the problem I see is, this male will not take a chance now. They must have thought a full attack by the six females would prevail. When the male realized that the females weren't winning, he came to kill us all. I was fortunate to kill the dominant female, though not as fortunate as if it had been the male. But this caused him to fall back. From here on, though, he'll be very cautious in his approach."

Lonato nodded as one of the scruffy dogs came by and sniffed him.

"We should protect the two dogs then. He must be aware that they warn us of their approach. It seems this wasn't a problem for them before, but surely the male will want to eliminate that disadvantage now."

"Yes, that's something we should do, as well as keeping the fires burning at night. Light seems to also be an advantage for us."

The dogs were brought closer to the village and as the day moved towards night the warriors and men of the village tried to prepare for another fight.

Torches were lit and as darkness settled, Orenda, Nazshoni, and Lonato walked out of the village and past the smoldering Lofa carcasses. They reached the edge of the ridge and Lonato held the torch up in an effort to see as far as possible.

"He's over there somewhere," Orenda said as he nodded to the where the cave would be. No sounds came from the area this time.

The darkness became complete, and only the fires and torches glowed. Soon after the night had set in, the male Lofa was heard growling.

Orenda lifted the musket to a ready position. Nazshoni placed an arrow in her bow and also watched closely.

The Lofa moved away from the cave but was traveling in a different direction. Orenda could hear it passing rapidly through the woods and darkness. Shortly after this, the dogs in the village were making sounds of distress. Orenda began jogging towards the village with Nazshoni behind. As he passed by Lonato, he spoke quickly.

"Stay here and keep the fires burning."

Lonato nodded as the warrior now picked up his pace. As Orenda and Nazshoni entered the village, the dogs were whimpering and moving about as if in pain.

Outside of the village and in the thick darkness, growls and strange sounds could be heard. The eerie noises floated about, and as Orenda moved towards one sound, another stirred in a different direction.

The foul smell of the creatures crept through the small community. Hakane approached Orenda and Nazshoni just as another strange screeching from the shadows pierced the night.

"What is this wicked thing they are preparing for us now?" Hakane asked.

Orenda nodded his uncertainty while searching the darkness.

The three moved cautiously towards the shaman's hut and found Jacey outside, also listening to the frightening sounds.

"I never thought I would live to hear something such as this." He turned to the others and seemed almost amused.

"What is it?" Nazshoni asked, as the screeching sounds slowly grew louder and could be heard from several directions.

"It's the 'blood song,' or that's what my grandfather called it. I'd all but forgotten his tales of the Lofa blood song. From what I remember of his stories, it means we're marked by the Lofa for death. I would suspect Orenda more so than the rest, but it has become a blood feud."

They watched the darkness with apprehension as the unsettling sounds continued to echo through the woodlands.

"There's more than just the male out there. I may not have killed the dominant female after all." Orenda said.

Jacey now spoke with reservation in his voice. "You may have, but the male must have at least one more female. I can't tell for certain how many there are, but you're right, there's surely more than one."

All through the night, the frightening sounds rang out. By daybreak, everyone was exhausted, and few had slept.

Onsi strolled back to the misty village. He propped his spear up against the hut he lived in. This wasn't his hut so much as it was his grandparent's hut. They had raised him from a young boy, and both had since passed away. He avoided going inside other than to sleep. It had never felt to be his real home.

As he sat wearily against the wall, he watched the men and warriors slowly walking in from their night of awaiting the Lofa. All appeared tired and hungry.

Orenda met up with Lonato who spoke in a solemn voice.

"This is a good strategy for those black-hearted devils. We've been awake and ready for battle all night. Now the Lofa will sleep while we try to recover."

Orenda nodded in agreement. He considered the comment and then replied.

"Perhaps the Lofa is not the only ones that can use the strategy. You and your men eat, try to get a little rest and then meet me at the ridge before midday." Orenda then walked over to Onsi.

"Come along Onsi; we have work to do, and we must do it quickly."

With some effort, Onsi stood up and followed behind the warrior, trying to keep up with him. Soon they found Nazshoni and all three went to Hakane's hut.

Chief Hakane and Jacey were outside of the hut talking. Orenda wasted no time.

"I believe we should return the favor and keep the Lofa awake today. It may help keep things balanced."

Hakane and Jacey looked at Orenda with a bit of puzzlement. Then, after a few seconds of thought, both realized what he spoke of and slight smiles broke over their faces. In a short time, the five were hurrying through the village giving instructions to the women.

Onsi was sent around to gather bones of any sort, especially those that were hollow. Any other hollow items that could be used were also gathered.

Some of the women were sent with Nazshoni. They gathered dried and also green grasses. They would then tie small bundles up with the green and dried grass intertwined.

Before midday Orenda, Nazshoni, and Onsi met up with Lonato and his warriors at the ridge.

Lonato examined the items they were carrying. The bones were tied together and rattled with much noise as Onsi and some of the village men handled them. He then commented.

"I think this is a dangerous thing you propose Orenda. Taking on the Lofa in battle is risky, but invading their cave is, well, much riskier."

Orenda appeared amused by Lonato's assertion.

"Yes, but I believe they'll not expect it. If we're cunning as well as brave, this will be a worthy task."

Lonato expressed agreement and after a few seconds replied, "we'll follow you."

The group moved with a purpose down the ravine and across the small valley. Then they began to climb a rocky ridge to reach the Lofa cave. Soon the putrid smell invaded their nostrils and assured them the creatures were close.

Lonato spoke softly to Orenda, "If those wretched beasts come out of the cave we'll all be dead. The Lofa will have all the advantage on this rocky hillside."

Trying to find a foothold, Orenda replied in an equally soft voice. "I think you're right my friend. And they won't need to kill us since we'll likely fall to our deaths trying to escape."

Cautiously the small band moved to a level area and could see the rough opening of a dark cave. Around the outside of the cave were many bones. Most were human, but some were of large animals. Onsi cringed inside as he was aware that these remains were of people he had known. He then spotted a large bear skull that had teeth marks on it. He moved carefully through the mass of bones in order not to make a sound.

Orenda pointed to a dead tree beside Onsi. He motioned to the higher branches.

Once Onsi began climbing, the warrior pointed to several other scrawny trees, indicating the other village men should climb and place the noise makers on the branches.

After all the noise makers had been placed in the trees and the men were down out of them, Lonato and the other warriors began lighting fire to the bundles of grass. While Onsi and the others quickly crawled to safety, Lonato, and his men tossed the bundles far into the cave.

When over half the bundles had been tossed in, Lonato motioned for his men also to begin leaving the area.

The bundles created a tremendous amount of smoke as they burned and the cave soon became thick with it.

From inside the gloomy cavern, growls and roars were heard. Meanwhile, Onsi and the village men could now be seen scampering towards the far ridge. Only Orenda, Nazshoni, and Lonato were left outside the entrance.

The Bitter Harvest

Orenda cocked his musket and aimed it into the cave as Nazshoni and Lonato lit and quickly tossed the last few bundles in as far as possible.

When the last one was tossed in, Nazshoni placed an arrow in her bow. Lonato also picked up his bow and readied it as the sounds of the Lofa grew stronger.

In the darkness and barely visible through the smoke, Orenda caught sight of a beast. It growled and moved about aggressively. He fired the musket, and a loud bang rang out, followed by smoke from the gunpowder.

The Lofa became silent and Orenda peered into the darkness to see if he'd hit the beast.

After standing outside the cave for a few moments as Orenda reloaded his musket, Lonato commented, "It seems we've woken them at the very least."

Orenda nodded and then turned to go back to the village. The breeze was now moving the noise makers about, and this caused the bones to rattle.

"Perhaps they'll get very little sleep as well," Orenda noted as they moved past them and swiftly made a departure from the area.

Chapter Seven: Bad to Worse

The village men and warriors all tried to sleep a bit more as the day progressed. Onsi checked on Kanuna several times but found the young warrior inactive and resting. Nazshoni stayed by his bedside much of the time, and Orenda also looked in on him throughout the day.

As the night crept closer, the village became active. Orenda moved about stirring everyone to a state of readiness. Torches were lit and weapons prepared.

Again the warrior moved to the ridge. He glanced back to see Nazshoni and Onsi. Lonato and several of his warriors were in the distance but also moving towards them. Further behind them were many torches and fires burning. A glow hovered over the area of the battlefield and village.

As darkness enveloped them, the Lofa were heard across the ravine as they moved out of the cave.

Orenda and the others peered into the night. The beasts then became strangely silent, though Orenda could hear them moving about in the brush and a few seconds later the creatures took off in separate directions.

"They've split up," Orenda said and tried to follow the sounds as one moved through the woods to his right, and another one, or possibly two moved in the opposite direction to the left side.

"We'll go with this one," Lonato said quickly and then took off towards the left of Orenda.

"Let's go," Orenda shouted and sprinted to his right with Nazshoni and Onsi trying to keep up.

In the darkness, the Lofa were perceived running through the rough terrain and towards the village. Onsi struggled with his torch and Nazshoni ran with an arrow in her bow. Orenda carried his musket in half ready position as all tried to keep track of the beast.

Soon they came to the village which was lit up by fires to keep the Lofa away. Several women were carrying torches and tending these fires. The dogs were whimpering and appeared petrified.

"Get inside!" Orenda yelled out to the women just as the male Lofa darted into the light. Before Orenda could get a good aim, the beast had grabbed one of the dogs and darted quickly into the dark woods.

Nazshoni let her snake arrow fly, and Onsi thought he saw it hit the male. A few seconds later the desperate yelps of the dog stopped.

The women dropped their torches and scurried towards the huts as Nazshoni retrieved another arrow from her quiver. Lonato and his men came into the village from a different direction.

"They're headed this way!" As Lonato yelled this out, another Lofa ran full speed from the darkness. It was dragging a large branch, and as it passed beside a fire, it pulled the branch through the blaze, causing embers and fire to fly everywhere.

Some of the women screamed. A dog moved about in the middle of the camp, appearing completely unnerved.

"The dog, get the dog!" Orenda yelled out. Onsi ran towards the dog as more embers and smoke filled the air.

Another Lofa came from a different direction. Before Onsi could reach the dog, the beast grabbed it. In this same instant, Nazshoni let her arrow fly, and it struck the Lofa in the side. The creature roared out in anger and slung the dog by the head, throwing it violently. The now dead dog landed on the chest of one of the village men and caused him to fly backward thus landing in another fire. Other men quickly helped the battered man out of the fire.

The Lofa was very close to Onsi, and he tried to back away. It roared, and as it did, several more arrows hit it. The creature began pulling these from its flesh and turned to run. Onsi glanced over to Nazshoni just as she let another arrow fly. The projectile landed in the Lofa's back as it disappeared into the darkness.

As the group reeled from this attack, the Male again crashed into the village from the darkness. Orenda again aimed the musket. This time, he fired a shot, but the beast moved too quickly, and the ball missed. The massive creature crashed into several huts causing horrible damage. Orenda sat his musket down and pulled his tomahawks out.

The male moved into the mass of men and took hold of two of them by the legs. The beast flung the screaming men around with little effort and slammed them to the ground, killing them instantly.

Orenda ran towards the male yelling out to get the creature away from the villagers. Nazshoni aimed her arrow in an attempt to get a shot, but now others were moving around the Lofa. It roared out again and ran straight over several unfortunate villagers; dragging the two dead men through fires, throwing more smoke and embers up into the air.

The beast then promptly ran full speed into the woods just as Orenda threw his tomahawk. The Lofa moved, and the shot landed in a tree. Nazshoni stepped up beside her husband with an arrow in her bow. She searched frantically for a visual on the beast in the hopes of landing a shot, but the creature had disappeared into the darkness.

Onsi stood in shock as he tried to realize the events that had just taken place. Women and children cried from inside the damaged huts. Logs from the scattered fires smoldered and burned across the entire area. Smoke and embers fluttered about as an indication of the chaos.

He gazed over the grounds and saw several dead men as well as the dead dog.

Few slept until dawn finally broke. Onsi had sat down and with the morning light finally closed his eyes to dose off for a few hours. Afterward he walked around the village and saw people cleaning up while others simply lay on the ground to rest.

As Onsi entered the hut where Kanuna was recovering, he found Nazshoni asleep with her head lying on the edge of her brother's bed. Kanuna also appeared to be sleeping. Orenda sat by a wall asleep, but awoke and glanced at Onsi briefly. Onsi went back outside and wondered around. The dogs were gone, and more men were lost. Everything seemed much darker, even in the daylight.

Later that day Orenda went to Hakane's hut. Soon Jacey also entered the small dwelling. The three men sat and smoked their pipes while in thought. Then Orenda spoke.

"Without the dogs, we'll be at a disadvantage. But we know they'll come again, so it changes little."

Hakane and Jacey nodded as they pulled draws from their pipes. Then Hakane replied.

"It seems they were also hungry. Taking the dogs would provide meat as well as put us at a disadvantage. But as it turned out they were set back by the fires. This may be why the male entered the village a second time to take two men. I suspect our best advantage still lay with the light of our fires. They attacked fast and tried to leave the light quickly."

Jacey nodded and added.

"We know they'll come. We're aware they'll have trouble in the light of the fires. This will be our edge. We should prepare the men for quick strikes and ensure we have the light on our side."

Orenda nodded and expelled a long stream of smoke as he considered the next battle.

As the day moved closer to night everyone prepared for the expected attack. Torches were made, and pits were dug to house more fires. The entire village worked without haste as Orenda walked here and there inspecting and suggesting changes or adjustments.

Chapter Eight: A Tear for the Brave

Tension grew with the setting sun. At dusk, Orenda and Nazshoni stood at the edge of the ravine. Onsi positioned himself behind them with a spear in one hand and a torch in the other.

Again the Lofa were heard stirring about in their cave. And as the darkness entrenched itself they came from the cavern and once again split up in different directions.

Orenda turned and yelled back to Lonato, "One is moving to the right and two to the left."

The warrior then took off at trotting speed to his right. He peered into the darkness to track the Lofa. Brush scratched against their legs as Nazshoni and Onsi followed behind.

The growls of the beast could be heard, and Onsi realized it was the large male they were tracking. Fear again tried to take hold of him, but he watched Orenda and resigned himself to follow the warrior even to death.

They arrived at the village as the male raced on the outskirts of the community, seeming reluctant to enter the light. Village men moved about nervously as they peered into the darkness, in anticipation of the Lofa striking hard and fast as the previous night.

The large fires in the village comforted Onsi as he and others moved with the sound of the creature in the woods. As he looked about at the frightened faces, he noticed Chief Hakane holding a large tomahawk as if also waiting for the beasts to arrive. The Chief had a stern face and appeared ready for battle. Little ways from him stood the Shaman Jacey holding his staff. He studied the darkness as well to keep track of the foul creatures.

Onsi felt confidence seeing his leaders. He gripped his spear tighter and moved with a renewed purpose.

Soon Lonato and his men arrived from the opposite side of the village as they also tracked Lofa. Several of the beasts could be heard moving about in the darkness.

"They may come in all at once. Stay alert!" As Orenda shouted this, he continued to move with the sounds of the beasts. It was evident he planned to be the first they would come to as he remained at the very edge of the firelight. He would raise his musket as the sounds grew in intensity and then lower it some as they moved away.

The night passed slow and distressful. A constant state of alertness wore the men down as the Lofa moved about in the darkness and always seemed on the verge of attack. As the dawn approached, they disappeared into the night and finally men began to sit and soon more than a few were fast asleep on the hard ground.

Orenda and Nazshoni went into the hut where Kanuna lay resting. Onsi sat down and was soon asleep himself. The day had moved past noon before he awoke.

Only a gray day presented itself as Onsi sat up and watched the activity of the village. It was strangely quiet and he then remembered the dogs were gone. He felt a pity in his heart for the scruffy animals that were perhaps taken for granted until now.

Orenda walked out of Kanuna's hut and moved towards Chief Hakane's. Onsi watched the warrior until he walked around another hut and out of sight.

The warrior found Hakane standing outside of his home. He gazed out over the village with an expression of concern.

"All of the men are growing weary," Hakane said as Orenda approached.

Orenda nodded. Then the two men noticed Jacey approaching. As the old shaman arrived, Orenda replied.

"The Lofa have fed, and perhaps they feel stronger now and less desperate. They also know they can do much damage, even though there appears to only be three left."

The men thought about this and Orenda continued.

"I don't understand why they didn't attack last night, though. What could they be waiting for?"

Again the men stood and considered the situation. Then Jacey looked out over the horizon. Orenda and Hakane noticed he was looking at something.

The shaman replied slowly, "They're waiting for that."

Orenda and Hakane turned around. Off in the distance was an approaching storm. Lightning could clearly be seen in the dark mass of clouds.

The men grimly observed this for several seconds. Then Orenda spoke.

"They just wanted to wear us down last night. With the rain coming we'll lose our last advantage of fire."

He turned back to the leaders and all three expressed a new concern as the day was almost gone and everything was prepared around a defense with light from the fires.

Then, Orenda appeared to think of something.

"Do you have drums and drum players?"

Hakane expressed confusion by this question.

"Yes, we do. They've not been used for a long time, though. We play them in ceremonies and celebrations. There's been no reason for either of these things since the Lofa arrived. Why do you ask?"

Orenda gazed back out to the storm as Hakane and Jacey waited for a reply.

"I think it is time for the Lofa to hear our blood song. This will be the final battle. Let's join with this storm and be proud with our song. The Lofa won't expect this."

Jacey and Chief Hakane looked at each other. Then they turned to Orenda and nodding in agreement smiled slightly. Hakane replied.

"We should work with swiftness and there is little time left."

The three moved quickly, stirring others to action. Jacey gathered all the drums and drum players together. Orenda and Hakane had dry torches brought into the huts. They also instructed others to prepare areas where small fires could be out of the rain. All worked with a sense of urgency as the storm and night moved in.

Nazshoni came to Orenda as fires were being lit.

"You should wear the paint husband. If this is the final battle, you should fight as a pure warrior."

Orenda said nothing but nodded.

The two went to Kanuna's hut, and with her brother watching sleepily, Nazshoni began to gently put the war paint on Orenda's face. Neither said anything, but they looked into each other's eyes again and again.

As he watched his wife, Orenda noticed a single tear well up and then roll softly down her cheek.

"Do you cry before the battle has been lost, my wife?"

Nazshoni continued to carefully apply the paint while considering his question. Finally, she spoke with a concerned voice.

"I cry because I know the battle will never end for us. I cry for the world that demands the blood of the brave so others can live free. And I cry because I love every day with you, no matter what comes our way. I know our days may be few, but my love for you will endure beyond time."

Orenda stared at Nazshoni with an expression of pain and love intermingled. He then gently reached up with his thumb and took the tear from her cheek. He softly placed the drop of moisture on his tongue and replied.

"I'll take this precious tear into battle then. With its power, I'm confident of victory."

Orenda then took the red paint from Nazhoni's hands. He put his thumb in it and reaching up, he painted a red line across his wife's eyes and nose. He nodded and smiled with satisfaction.

Nazshoni smiled as well and then embraced her husband.

Kanuna also smiled as he witnessed this, but then grimaced in pain. He turned his head and fell back to sleep as a small fire crackled in the fireplace.

When Orenda stepped from the hut, the skies had become darker, and the smell of rain was in the air. The wind blew Nazshoni's hair about as they stood looking over the village.

Orenda picked up his tomahawks and Nazshoni took her bow and quiver of arrows from the side of the hut. All eyes were on these two warriors as thunder sounded in the distance.

Drums and drummers sat ready, and the fires whipped about in the wind. Women, as well as some older children, stood with the drummers holding sticks that would make loud clicking sounds.

The warriors began walking until they reached the middle of the village where Orenda stopped. He looked over all of the people before speaking. Thunder again rolled, and several rain drops landed on them. Finally, the warrior spoke.

"The Lofa will come tonight. We'll have difficulty keeping the fires lit. So the drums will keep the fire burning inside our spirits. Once the Lofa attack, the drums should start and not cease until the battle is won. No matter what, play the song of victory. It will let the Lofa know that we intend to win this battle..."

Once again he looked them over. Once again the lightning and thunder accented his words. As more rain came down and as the darkness took over the day, he spoke the final words.

"This is an honorable fight. If we die tonight, we'll die an honorable death. But I say to all of you; let's have the Lofa die tonight and save our honorable death for another day and another battle. Are you with me?"

A loud roar erupted from the group, and the women chanted and tapped their sticks together. A new confidence flowed through the community and as the storm moved in, Onsi felt a strong desire to fight to the last, no matter what; a death in this battle would be one with dignity.

Chapter Nine: Black Eyes of Death

Again Orenda, Nazshoni, and Onsi moved to the edge of the ridge. The wind whipped sporadic rain drops onto their skin and Onsi struggled to hold the torch in a manner that would keep it burning.

Shortly, the Lofa emerged from the cave. Their growls and howls were much stronger and filled with an air of violence. They want blood, Onsi thought. A chill ran down his spine, and he again struggled with a growing fear inside.

Orenda and Nazshoni strained to see across the ravine as lightning briefly revealed the area. Darkness quickly sat back in, and only the fierce howls could be heard.

The beasts began moving at a rapid pace towards the village. Nazshoni pulled the arrow in her bow to a ready position. Orenda put his wrists through leather straps on his tomahawks. These would keep him from losing the weapons in battle. He held them down and in a ready position as he and Nazshoni began to move in a direction to intercept the beasts.

Sounds of heavy Lofa feet hitting the earth could be heard now and almost felt. Lonato and his men had also arrived and now stood firm in the path of the creatures.

Lighting again lit up the area and the large male with two smaller females could be seen running straight towards them. Darkness immediately took over after the brief glimpse. Onsi waited for the beasts to run into them. Several seconds tensely passed.

"Where are they?" Lonato shouted in a bewildered voice, as thunder rumbled overhead.

They all strained to see in the night. Again a small burst of lightning allowed a brief glance ahead. The Lofa were not to be seen.

"They must be going through the woods!" Orenda shouted and quickly darted towards the village with the others falling in behind him.

With the brush and ground damp from the rain, the creatures moved with speed and stealth through the foliage.

Upon reaching the edge of the village, Onsi heard the drums begin to play, and the women began to chant while striking the sticks together.

A scene of carnage developed in front of them as a female Lofa brutally rampaged through the community, running over people and raking tree limbs through the struggling fires. Embers again cascaded into the air, but still the drummers played, and the women chanted.

An arrow from Nazshoni's bow whizzed past Onsi's ear and landed on the back of the Lofa. It roared and turned to find Orenda charging it at full speed. The beast raised its arm to strike as Orenda attacked.

Another female now entered in from a different direction and rampaged through the area with equal ferocity. It then disappeared just as quickly into the darkness.

As this happened, Orenda swung the tomahawk in his right hand and landed a blow in the forearm of the creature he fought. He then swung the tomahawk in his left hand, and this blow landed on the back of the large female. It roared and immediately grappled fiercely with the warrior.

Lightning and the few remaining fires presented the deadly struggle to Onsi as he tried to move closer. His torch was barely flickering now, and he tossed it down to take a better hold of his spear. Across the way, he could make out Lonato and his men battling one of the females. It crashed into a hut and ran into the darkness as the drums continued to play the rhythmic song of death or victory.

The female battling Orenda was almost on top of him now. He had placed one of the tomahawks into the chest of the beast and with much difficulty was keeping its claws from ripping into him.

Nazshoni moved past Onsi and let another arrow fly into the foul creature. She quickly pulled another from her quiver.

The Lofa jerked in pain and then ran away towards the edge of the village and the darkness. Orenda began to stand up as Nazshoni tried to get another shot in at the retreating female.

Unexpectedly, and from behind them, the large male ran past Onsi at full speed. He immediately smelled the stench as it went by. The male grabbed Orenda's leg as the warrior was attempting to stand and then pulled him at full speed through the village and out the other side.

Nazshoni screamed out and ran after them. Before she could catch up, the two females came back into the fray from the darkness; blocking her path with another violent rampage.

Without much thought, Onsi had begun to run behind Nazshoni when the Lofa females entered with a determination to create havoc and block anyone from following the male. Men went flying about, and fires were stirred and spread around, throwing embers once again into the sky. Thunder and lightning erupted. The rain came down upon everything and still the drums played.

Onsi fell away just as a female ran past, almost running over him. Nazshoni stood in the middle of the chaos firing arrows one after another into the beasts. Lonato grabbed a branch from a partially burning fire and attempted to slow one of the creatures down.

In this dark fog of battle, Onsi's mind grappled with the ferocity of the events around him, and he tried to think of what to do. He stood up and took his spear in his hands, holding it the way Orenda had instructed him to.

Women continued to chant their song and tap their sticks. One of the female Lofa grabbed an unfortunate woman and threw her across the area. Still, the others continued bravely in a strange mix of violence and music.

Nazshoni landed an arrow in the side of this female directly after she threw the woman. The Lofa roared out and noticing Nazshoni; it took off straight for her.

Onsi felt it would tear the bow woman apart. He began to run, hoping to intercept the creature. Nazshoni landed another arrow into the beasts' chest. It slowed but continued towards her.

Onsi's heart beat faster and his legs moved quicker. He held the spear tight. Nazshoni reached back to pull another arrow from her quiver. She wouldn't have time, but she didn't move from her spot.

Just as the beast was about to overrun the bow woman, Onsi's spear jabbed into its side. With the momentum he'd gained, he and the Lofa both slid away from Nazshoni.

Onsi landed almost on top of the retched creature. His face was nearly touching the face of the Lofa. The breath stunk so badly; he immediately became nauseous.

Before he could try to get away from the injured beast, it rolled over and pinned him down. It growled and opened its large mouth. Onsi realized it intended to bite his head off. He grimaced and prepared himself for the beheading.

As the creature was aiming to land its bite on Onsi, he saw an arm swing down and onto the back of the Lofa's head. Its eyes expressed shock as it reared up and grunted. He now saw that Nazshoni had jumped onto its back and stabbed her knife into the back of its skull. She held onto the knife and the Lofa as it turned and grunted again while flaying its arms in vain back towards Nazshoni.

Onsi found himself freed from the beast as it continued to move about violently in death troughs. He slid away in the mud and rain. Nazshoni rode the beast down until it finally landed face first into the drenched earth. She pulled her knife from the Lofa's skull, glanced over at Onsi and seeing he was all right, she smiled. Onsi smiled back to her but had the strangest feeling about doing so in the midst of this damp, miserable carnage.

With little haste, Nazshoni jumped back into action and ran towards the other beast that was fighting Lonato and his group. The drums played on as Onsi attempted to stand.

Meanwhile, in the woods, Orenda was being dragged violently by one leg. He struggled to keep his other leg from being twisted and broken. The large male Lofa grunted and moved with purpose through the darkness.

The warriors' leather breeches protected him some, but he could feel his back being scratched up from the rough ground. He tried to spot anything to help him as lightning briefly lit the sky up.

Then, after being pulled some distance from the village, he caught a glimpse of an approaching tree. He turned his tomahawk in a ready position, and as he moved past the tree, he hooked the tomahawk head to it.

A violent and painful jerk pulled him free from the Lofa's grasp. He quickly got to his feet as the male beast stumbled from the sudden jolt, but then turned back towards him.

Orenda could scarcely see the creature as darkness and rain loomed all around. He listened carefully and realized the male Lofa breathed with a rasp in his lungs. The warrior now became wise to the fact that one of Nazshoni's snake arrows must have hit its mark. The beast was sick. This would give the warrior a slight advantage.

He held his tomahawks out and in a ready position. Lightning revealed the massive creature in front of him. It was watching him and appeared ready to strike.

Thunder rolled above the two and rain dripped from Orenda's face. The Lofa charged him. Orenda stepped aside and swung his tomahawk. The blow barely made contact, but the warrior felt it hit flesh as the beast slid by him.

Again the warrior took a defensive stance as he tried to spot the male in the darkness. Again he listened for the ragged breath. Just as he located it, the Lofa charged again.

Almost face to face with the beast, Orenda had to fall and roll away as its claws were reaching out to remove his arm.

Once again lightning allowed the warrior to spot his foe as he regained his footing. Thunder continually rolled through the air. In the distance, Orenda heard the drums playing. He felt glad to know the other two creatures had not leveled the village. With a new strength, he braced himself for the next strike.

Inside the village, Lonato and his men surrounded the remaining female. It would strike out and throw one of the men violently through the air. But Lonato or another warrior would strike a tomahawk blow when it did so, causing the creature to roar and move back.

Nazshoni moved up and immediately began sending arrows into the beast. With this new attack, the Lofa charged through the men and straight for Nazshoni. She fired an arrow into its leg, and it fell. She backed up as she quickly pulled another from her quiver and strung it in her bow.

The Lofa stood up and charged again. Nazshoni began moving backward through the village. A spear from one of the village men flew from behind the Lofa, missing it and landing beside Nazshoni. She again fired an arrow into the beast, but it continued in a desperate bid to kill the bow woman before collapsing. The drums played without ceasing as she retreated through the huts.

Nazshoni once again reached back for an arrow as the beast closed in on her. She had no more, and she realized she had now become cornered between two huts. The creature was almost on her. She pulled the knife from her moccasin boot and prepared for the final struggle.

The large beast stood up straight, its black eyes glimmered as it raised its arm to tear through Nazshoni. Then, something hit it from behind. It turned, and Nazshoni could see a tomahawk buried in its back.

The beast roared out, and again something struck it. The creature staggered back. Lighting lit the area up, and Nazshoni saw Kanuna outside the door of his hut. He was taking aim with another tomahawk. The Lofa took a step as if wanting to attack him. Kanuna reared back and let the tomahawk fly. This one landed square in the beasts' face.

Nazshoni now moved away from the creature as it stood briefly in the grip of death. As the massive Lofa began to fall back, Nazshoni saw her brother also fall to the ground.

Lonato and the others moved quickly to ensure the beast did not rise again. Nazshoni ran to Kanuna. She picked him up in her arms.

"Kanuna, Kanuna!" She began to cry.

Her brother opened his eyes and smiled slyly.

"Did you think I was going to miss out on this fight?" He said with a feeble voice.

She laughed and hugged him. She rocked him back and forth, crying and laughing at the same time.

Onsi came to her.

"Help him back to bed. I've got to find my husband."

Onsi nodded and began to help Kanuna back inside.

The rain came to a stop as she was standing up. She wiped her face and ran in the direction Orenda had been dragged away by the male Lofa. Lonato came to her as she moved to the edge of the village.

"He was taken this way," Lonato said and immediately Nazshoni took off into the darkness. Lonato barely had time to start running to keep up with her.

Through the brush and around trees they went. Thunder and lighting erupted overhead and lit the way for the two warriors. Soon Nazshoni slowed down some and Lonato was able to catch up.

As Lonato arrived beside her, he noticed they were at the edge of a small valley. When lighting lit the area up, he could see Orenda and the male Lofa below as they faced each other in battle.

Nazshoni immediately reached back for an arrow, only to find again that she had no more. She quickly reached down and pulled the knife from her boot. As she started to move towards her husband, Lonato grabbed her arm.

"No, Nazshoni, you'll only distract him. He's focused now; this is his battle, you must allow him to finish it."

The woman warrior moaned, as if in agony. She struggled briefly. Then, seeming to realize Lonato was right, she began to cry softly."

The Lofa charged Orenda once again. And again Orenda fell away just in time and was barely able to regain his footing before the beast turned and came at him again. He jumped back from this attack and managed to land another blow from the tomahawk into the Lofa's arm.

Orenda knew well that the creature would catch him sooner or later. He searched the area frantically every time lightning brought a brief view of the surrounding woods. Finally, as the beast was about to charge again, he spotted what he'd been searching for.

Two trees were growing close together and formed a large 'V' shape. After spotting this, he had to move again quickly as the Lofa came at him. This time the male stretched its arms and claws out as it was anticipating Orenda would fall away. The warrior couldn't gain enough distance, and the claws of the beast inflicted three large gashes on Orenda's upper right arm.

Nazshoni gasped in fright as her husband growled in anger and pain. Lonato again held her from running to him.

As Orenda stood back up and glanced towards his bleeding arm, he also began to move to his left. The Lofa watched him and moved to keep the warrior to his front. The beast roared and growled almost at the same time as lighting lit the battleground for a few seconds.

Carefully, Orenda moved and glanced back to help him position himself. The Lofa moved back and forth on all fours, and Orenda knew he only had a few seconds before the beast charged again.

Rain began to fall once more. Thunder rolled above and as Orenda found the position he'd been maneuvering towards, lighting lit up the skies.

The Lofa charged with a determination to catch Orenda as he fell in one direction or the other.

Orenda waited until the last second. Rather than fall away, as the beast expected, he raised both tomahawks in front of him, and this extended his reach. The sharp points at the end of the tomahawks landed in the beast's chest, and Orenda rolled backward. It was a tried and true maneuver he'd learned as a young boy. He lifted his legs into the crotch area of the beast and the Lofa tumbled over the top of him.

The beast grunted with surprise and pain. But the extraordinary shock came as it flew backward and directly into the 'V' shape of the trees. The male Lofa suddenly found that it was lodged in-between the two trees, and as Orenda flipped back up, the creature struggled and growled out in pain and anger.

The huge male was upside down and wedged in a trap. It stared at Orenda as he cautiously approached. It pressed against the trees, and the warrior could see the beast would soon break free.

As Orenda moved closer to the beast, Nazshoni laughed slightly in relief and the fortunate change of circumstances. Lonato also expelled a breath of contentment.

The vicious black eyes of the male Lofa flashed as it struggled and stared at the warrior. As it was about to break lose from its entrapment in the trees, Orenda spoke with a firm voice.

"I'm sending you back to the hell you came from and setting these people free. Tell the demons where you're headed to that they're not welcome here either."

The beast growled and struggled again with an immense effort. Orenda swung the tomahawk with a violent force and landed the blow directly on the forehead of the Lofa. It groaned and gurgled as the life force expelled from it.

Again lightning blazed across the sky, revealing the battlegrounds. Then the thunder rolled, seeming to accentuate Orenda's victory.

Lonato now let Nazshoni lose, and she ran swiftly to her husband. Orenda turned and caught her in his arms as she wept and laughed at the same time. Lonato came to them and nodded in a gesture of tribute as the rain continued falling on all three.

They followed the sounds of the drums back to the village, and as the three walked wearily into the community, the drums slowly stopped. Everyone stared at the three in anticipation.

Lonato raised Orenda's hand in the air and shouted out, "Victory is ours!"

Immediately a shout of joy rang out in a tremendous expression of relief and triumph.

Chapter Ten: Storm Rider

The following morning Onsi walked out of his hut to find a scene of carnage and devastation. Homes were damaged and broken down. The dead Lofa caused the area to stink terribly. Smoldering logs from the fires lay scattered in disarray and created a smoky haze all around the village.

Yet, Onsi had a sense of peace that he'd not felt for many months. As the people of the community awoke and began cleaning up, he observed an immediate change. There were laughter and smiles. Everyone appeared relieved that death by the Lofa was no longer in their future.

Onsi walked into Kanuna's hut. He found the young warrior sitting up and smiling. Nazshoni had a smile on her face as well, and Orenda stood by with an expression of joy.

"Well, there is the hero now," Kanuna said as Onsi closed the door.

"Hero," Onsi's mind was still a blur, and he wasn't sure what Kanuna was talking about.

"As if you don't know," Kanuna chuckled and continued.

"I heard how you took on the Lofa with a spear and saved my sister's life."

Now the events of the previous night slowly returned to his mind. Onsi hadn't thought of the event as heroic.

"I just did what needed to be done." He said rather meekly, but with a conviction that it was the truth he spoke.

Orenda walked up to him and patted his back, "Spoken like a true warrior."

"Warrior," Onsi asked?

The young man struggled with the thought. Now as he stood in front of these three warriors, he realized that they were also not immune to fear. He remembered the feeling that flowed through him as he ran towards the Lofa that was charging Nazshoni. And he remembered his thoughts. He knew he might die, and this frightened him, but it would be defending someone he cared for, and it would be an honorable death. He now knew that this must be the same thoughts of these three warriors every time they do battle.

"Yes, warrior," Nazshoni said softly and then continued; "do you suppose a fisherman would attack a Lofa in that way?"

"I guess I've never thought of myself as a warrior," Onsi replied.

The three now watched him as if observing a deep change taking place inside the young man at that very instant. After some additional thought, he spoke again.

"Well, if that's true, then maybe one day I could travel with you three. I have no one left here and I'm going to miss you very much when you leave."

They glanced at each other when Onsi said this. Silence held the room for several long seconds. Finally, Orenda spoke.

"You should consider your words well Onsi. You've seen the way we live. It'll also be the way we die. And death may come sooner than later. What you ask is a serious thing."

Onsi nodded and smiled slightly. He then excused himself and went to clean the stench of the Lofa from his body.

Later that day, Orenda and Lonato stood watching on as a very reluctant horse was being made to pull one of the dead Lofa from the village.

"My father will want to meet you," Lonato said, turning to Orenda.

The warrior nodded. "I would be honored to meet your father."

The Bitter Harvest

Lonato continued. "I believe he would also like to see the male Lofa before the corpses are burned if you don't mind waiting."

Orenda nodded again, "We'll wait to burn them."

The following day the villagers continued to clean up and bury their dead. Onsi, Nazshoni, and Orenda talked with Kanuna, and were very pleased that the young warrior was mending well.

The morning after, Lonato and others from his tribe visited the small village. Orenda, Chief Hakane, and the other elders met the visitors as they rode slowly through the community.

On a large horse sat a man that was immediately recognized as being important. His dress was of a leader and he rode in the front.

Once dismounted, Lonato came up beside the man as he stood in front of Orenda, Chief Hakane, and Jacey.

"Father, this is the warrior Orenda." He motioned to Orenda and then continued. "Orenda, this is my father, Chief Taima."

Orenda was surprised by this but quickly recovered and bowed slightly. Further behind them, Nazshoni was also rather amazed to find that Lonato was the son of a chief. She smiled to herself as the leaders and visitors greeted each other.

"It is an honor Sir," Orenda said.

Chief Taima then greeted Hakane and the others. After which, he turned back to Orenda.

"I apologize for sending so few warriors Orenda. We did, however, send our best."

Orenda nodded and replied with obvious respect. "The help you sent was sufficient."

Chief Taima and those with him walked around the battle areas and inspected the Lofa corpses. His son Lonato relayed the events of the battles as they had occurred.

Later the corpses were burned and the night sky was filled with the smoke of the raging fires.

During Chief Taima's visit, a celebration was arranged for the following week.

Kanuna continued to recover and by the time the celebration took place he was able to attend though having to remain sitting due to his mending leg.

It was a beautiful festival and the likes of which Onsi had not seen in this community for a very long time. As the fires began to burn down and after the feast; as well as much music and dancing, Chief Taima began to speak.

"We've prepared some gifts for our new friends, Orenda, Nazshoni, and Kanuna."

The visiting tribe then brought one by one some special items. For Orenda, a new and very well crafted breast plate. It was ornately decorated and would be very expensive to barter for.

Nazshoni received a new bow and arrow quiver, filled with arrows. The bow was obviously of a very high quality, and Nazshoni appeared to almost cry when she held it.

Kanuna received two very high-quality tomahawks with iron heads. They were also nicely decorated and painted.

Last of all came a very special gift from Chief Taima. He stood in front of all and spoke with a loud voice.

"Orenda, you've been a vital part in saving this tribe and the surrounding lands from the vicious Lofa. After hearing about your battle with the male Lofa, I wish to bestow upon you the title of 'Orenda, The Storm Rider.' This name will be heralded as far north, south, east, and west, as our tribe has influence. Your battle scars from the male Lofa will be the honor marks others will know you by. My request to all other tribes will be that you are treated with generosity, respect, and honor."

Orenda expressed tremendous gratitude, and the celebration began to subside slowly, yet still lasted long into the night.

As Kanuna healed, many other gifts were bestowed upon the three warriors. The women of the village made several sets of buckskin clothing for them. Nazshoni was astounded when she received some expertly crafted tops and trousers in the fashion of her role as a warrior.

Orenda and Kanuna also received well-crafted clothing among other gifts from the village. While they remained within the community, all three were treated as heroes and with much gratitude.

The day slowly arrived for the warriors to leave. Kanuna had healed completely and early in the morning the three began preparing their pack horses.

Onsi came to them; obviously distraught.

"I've not looked forward to this day. I realize you must go, but I wish you didn't have to."

The three stopped their work and glanced at each other. Orenda then spoke.

"Onsi, if you would like, we would be proud to have you travel with us."

When Orenda said this, Onsi's eyes grew wide. He replied with a nervous voice.

"Are you sure? Do you mean that?"

They smiled, and Orenda said, "Yes, we've already talked about it, and we are sure, as long as you are sure. It won't be an easy life, though. You should be certain, this is what you wish to do."

Onsi replied without hesitation, "I'm very certain." He paused briefly in thought and then went on. "Before I met the three of you, it was as if my life had little meaning. I promise you; I will not be a burden. Just let me gather my things."

He then quickly went to pack. Orenda, Nazshoni, and Kanuna smiled at each other and returned to their tasks.

Later, as the sun approached the mid-day sky, the four mounted their horses and prepared to leave. The entire village said their goodbyes and they slowly moved out of the small community.

As the small group ventured farther away, they reached a point that Onsi knew the last place he could look back and see the village that had been his home. He stopped his horse and turned to the now distant group of huts.

The others stopped when they realized he had halted.

"If you don't mind me asking, just where is it that we're going to?" Onsi inquired.

Orenda replied as his horse moved anxiously under him.

"West. It is where we were headed before you found us. Beyond the great river is a tribe that has asked for our help. They're being tormented by giants."

Onsi's face grimaced slightly, "giants?"

He glanced again at the distant village. Orenda turned his horse back west and replied, "Yes, giants."

Kanuna also began moving west again, behind Orenda. Finally, Nazshoni spoke, "Come along Onsi... You've battled a pack of Lofa; surely you're not afraid of a few giants."

The woman warrior then turned her horse and began moving west as well.

Onsi replied quickly, "No, I'm not afraid of a few giants." He glanced back at the village one more time, then continued, softly and under his breath, "Not much anyway."

Immediately Nazshoni shouted back, "I heard that," as her horse maneuvered over some rocks.

Onsi became quite surprised by this, "You heard that? How did you hear that?"

Nazshoni laughed.

It was a beautiful laugh and the first time Onsi had heard her laugh with joy this way. He instantly smiled and prodded his horse to catch up with the others.

At the front of the group, Orenda had also smiled due to Nazshoni's laughter. It was a good omen he thought to himself. To start their next adventure on the heels of Nazshoni's beautiful laughter was a very good thing indeed.

The End

We hope you enjoyed The Bitter Harvest. You may be interested in other books by Oliver Phipps. As a bonus feature, a preview of his book "Tears of Abandon" has been included here.

In this haunting adventure, several friends from college put together a plan to kayak down an Alaskan River during the summer break. Soon there are five young people headed for the Alaskan wilderness. Things go great until they discover an unusual sound and begin to follow it.

We hope you enjoy the following preview of Tears of Abandon, by Oliver Phipps.

Oliver Phipps

Tears of Abandon

© 2014 Oliver Phipps All rights reserved
Copyright

Chapter One: A Daring Plan

Their faces appeared stern, as if weathered by a sheer force of purpose. The shovels, picks, and other articles of life that could be seen around them presented an apparent effort for daily survival. Drew examined the fellows in the old black and white photos with a discerning interest he hadn't done before. He studied their grizzled beards; their coarse clothing, and the harsh woodland that hovered all around. Somehow, these men had taken on nature and held the wilderness at bay with crude tools of a bygone day and will power alone.

Drew tried to visualize himself in the picture. Perhaps somewhere in the background, standing with a pick in hand, maybe by the large sluice box; or kneeling by the stream with a gold pan, having just picked up a container full of Gods' essential element. He tried to imagine himself hiking up the forest covered hills with a backpack and a walking staff. But he just couldn't see himself enduring such hardships for very long, no matter how hard he tried. He knew he didn't have a physical stature built for an extended stay in the rugged environment of Alaska and he wouldn't attempt to deceive himself into thinking such a thing.

He closed the large book and laid it back on the coffee table in front of him. Picking up his drink he scanned the front again. The title indicated something to do with the Alaskan Gold rush in pictures.

He gazed across the coffee table at his roommate Richard, who he's called Rich for as long as he can remember. Rich had the rugged features of an outdoorsman; the unruly locks of brown hair and square jaw. He could picture Rich in Alaska, by a stream with a gold pan in hand.

He and Rich had been best friends through high school and entered college together. Rich had always been the more outgoing of the two. While they both suited up for the high school football team, Rich played and Drew warmed the bench. Drew admired his friend's physical prowess. Drew just always seemed to be the semi-nerd, or brains of the duo. While Rich inclined more towards the muscles persona in their friendship.

The sound of rock music crept back to his senses and the several drinks he had already drunk began to take full effect; he looked at Jack as he leaned on the armrest talking to Rich. Jack certainly fit his image of a confident and well to do guy. Drew had come to regard that confidence as a thinly disguised arrogance, however.

Jack came from a wealthy family and there would be no doubt he would stroll into a CEO position somewhere after graduation. The cushy life Jack had laid before him didn't bother Drew so much as the position he'd taken between himself and Rich over the last few years. Jack and Rich both retained a zeal for adventure. Jack took a shine to Rich in their first year of college and since that time he'd become a wedge, slowly splitting Drew and his best friend apart.

Although he, Rich, Jack and Cindy; Jack's girlfriend, were all in their early twenties, there had always seemed to be a separation and hierarchy between them due to financial standing. Drew casually scanned Jack's apartment and found no difficulty noticing the difference. The living room of Jack's apartment would hold the entire apartment he and Rich shared. Rich had become very fond of Jack and Cindy's little drinking and socializing parties, but Drew had begun to enjoy them less and less.

"So Drew, you in or not?" Jack turned to Drew as his conversation with Rich found a stopping point.

"Yeah Drew, what's it going to be, you in?" Rich sounded like someone who'd been put off as long as he cared to be.

"Well, you know guys; Alaska seems to be a pretty dangerous place if you ask me." Drew cringed a little inside as this came out more sheepishly than he'd intended.

"Ohhh," Jack wailed in the condescending tone Drew had become accustom to. "You hear that Cindy." Jack turned and spoke in a voice loud enough to carry over the music. "Alaska is a dangerous place!" Cindy sat at the bar directly behind Rich watching a show on TV.

"What are you saying about me? You know I'm trying to watch this show Jack."

Jack now began to show his level of intoxication. Drew felt the only reason to get Cindy involved would be to make Drew appear weak.

Cindy and Jack had become a couple the first year of school and Jack had encouraged her to find someone for Rich in an apparent attempt to corner Rich's friendship. Though she found several available girls over the course of their schooling, Rich didn't seem able to hold onto one.

But, since Drew never actually had a real girlfriend before, he often found himself in a position of the third wheel. Even his prom date was more of a mutual agreement than an actual date. The so called "date" was a girl who didn't function well with the opposite sex either.

Regardless of this, he refused to let Jack take over his friendship with Rich. On the other hand, Rich seemed oblivious to what Drew perceived as a straightforward attempt by Jack to push him out of the picture.

Jack turned back to Drew and continued. "You know Drew, this is 1992 not 1892. Things have changed since the gold rush days in those pictures. I hear Alaska has electricity and even running water now."

Drew now pushed his glasses back up on his nose in what had become something of a nervous habit.

"Come on Drew it'll be fun, you can hang out with Cindy if you like," Jack now spoke with a stifled laugh.

"Hey, I heard my name again. What are you setting me up for," Cindy said with some frustration as she glanced at them from behind the bar.

"I know Drew, you can ask that new girl to come along," Rich jumped into the conversation with an increasingly rare intercession.

"New girl," exclaimed Jack, appearing very much in the mood to belittle Drew in a manner thinly disguised as buddy jokes. "I don't recall there ever being any old girls; much less a new one Rich?" Jack smirked again as he then finished his drink.

"You remember that girl Ashley he dated for a while Jack?"

Drew recalled the friend he used to know as Rich made an obvious attempt to keep some of the heat off of him. But he felt Jack would take every advantage at this point.

"Actually Rich, I only went out with Ashley one time." Drew again felt his reply sounded weak.

"There you go then, once is enough for me, so this girl is the new girl then,"

quiet surprisingly Jack took an about face.

Regardless of this, Drew didn't want to bring Beth into the conversation; particularly a somewhat alcohol infused one. He and Beth met in the college library a few weeks before the semester ended. Due to what he considered the somewhat rough nature of his friends, he intentionally kept their dates a secret.

After two months of this quiet relationship with Beth, Rich discovered Drew was dating a girl. So, with the secret out, Drew had invited her to come by the apartment sometime so she could meet his friends.

"Well, maybe I can mention the trip to her when I see her again." He hoped this might move the subject away from Beth.

"Yeah Drew, and tell this 'new girl' the trip is all expenses paid, so she needn't worry about spending school money or money for those girlie things she may need." Drew gazed across the coffee table at Jack and wondered if he could actually be making an attempt to be nice or simply implying the only girls Drew could date would be the ones with little money.

"Sure, yes I'll tell her Jack. Thanks again for the offer. I'm getting a bit tired so if you'll excuse me, I believe I'll head back to the apartment."

"Yeah all right, just go ahead and leave when things are picking up," Jack snickered again indicating he'd not finished with Drew yet and wished to get one more snide remark in.

On the way back to the apartment he and Rich shared, Drew smiled slightly as he thought about Beth. She had that girl next door beauty, with brown hair that flowed around in a free sort of way. She stood about five foot five inches and seemed to prefer wearing shoes that would help her stand a few inches taller. She always glowed with enthusiasm and he couldn't remember a time that she'd been upset about anything. He recalled how nervous he became before asking her out on a date the day they met.

Then he chuckled a little when he thought of what he told her. On their third date he brought up that she sometimes had a 'sad smile.' She giggled and told him there wasn't such a thing. Only Beth could get her cute little mouth to make a pouty twist that way. Drew couldn't think of any other way to describe the unique expression. This seemed to be a special Beth characteristic and he loved that about her.

The next morning Drew crawled out of bed, prepared for a usual Saturday morning. After a routine visit to the bathroom he went to the small area they called the kitchen.

Rich had come in sometime during the night but Drew had no idea when. After a light breakfast he sat down to watch some TV. No sooner had he switched the television on the phone rang.

"Hello?"

"Hi Drew! How are you?" He knew the voice and immediately his demeanor improved upon hearing Beth on the other end.

"Well, I'm doing all right. I was just, ah, watching some cartoons." He wanted to be a little more humorous; Rich told him girls wanted their guys to make them laugh occasionally. Beth did laugh at the cartoon answer and Drew smiled. He even surprised himself at being able to make a witty comment that early in the morning.

"Do you think I could come by and see you today?"

Drew scanned the apartment trying to estimate how much time he needed to get the place half way clean.

"Sure, that would be great Beth. I thought about you last night and how I'd enjoy seeing you sometime this weekend."

"Yeah, I thought the same thing," she replied happily. "How about forty-five minutes or so, would that be all right?"

"Yeah, that would be great," he immediately began picking up some dirty laundry from the floor. "Do you want me to meet you somewhere to make sure you get here all right?"

"Nah, that's okay, I'm sure I know where the apartment is. Could you give me the number again though, just to make sure I remember it right?"

"211."

"All right, that's what I thought. I'll see you soon, bye."

"Okay, see you soon then, bye."

What might be called a cleaning tornado ensued immediately after Drew hung up. He hid dirty dishes, crammed dirty clothes in the closet, and tried to camouflage stains on the end table. He jumped in the shower, dropped the soap several times, and spilled half the bottle of shampoo in an attempt to finish in three minutes.

Glancing at the clock as he dressed and brushed his hair Drew felt confident he would be ready in time, but the chime of the door bell dispelled this notion. With no socks or shoes on Drew strolled through the living room scanning around to be sure the small apartment would be presentable. Opening the door, sunshine streamed in around the wide smile and shapely silhouette of Beth.

"Hi, I hope you didn't have plans or anything, I just thought if you weren't busy…"

"No, no I had a lazy day planned. I'm glad you called," Drew opened the door to let her in. He noticed Beth cradled a book close to her chest as she might a purse or something valuable.

"Please have a seat anywhere."

Beth sat down and Drew took a seat across from her. "I'm really glad you came to visit Beth."

"I'm umm, glad you're glad I came to visit," she said with a little giggle. "Do I need to take my shoes off?"

This puzzled Drew and he glanced down at her feet. She had a nice pair of sandals on and her toenails were painted a crimson red.

"I don't know. Do you want to take your shoes off?" as the awkwardness between the two became more apparent.

"Well, I just thought maybe because of the carpet or something," she then nodded at his feet. Drew looked down and realized in the rush he'd forgotten to put socks or shoes on.

"Oh, no, I see what you mean; no I just wanted to let you in and forgot I'd not put my socks or shoes on." They both laughed which seemed to relieve some of the awkward tension.

"What do you have there?" Drew pointed to the book.

"Oh, this is Candace Clarendon's' new mystery 'River Boat.' I just love her mysteries. I've always got one of her books with me. In fact, there have been times that one of her books has been the only thing to keep me from being alone." Beth giggled a little as if she'd told a secret. "Have you read any of her books?"

"Umm," Drew struggled to recall any of her books he'd ever read. "I did read some of her book 'Desert Flower.'" This had some truth to it as he'd picked the book up in a store once and flipped through the pages reading bits and pieces.

"I love that one," Beth seemed to get excited now, sitting up straighter as if ready to get into a deep discussion on the matter. "I would love to be able to write the way Candace does." She now took a very serious tone. Drew realized this must be important to her and in an effort to avoid talking in-depth about "Desert Flower" yet remain on subject; he took the opportunity to encourage her.

"You could do that, I'm sure you could."

"What, you really think I could write like Candace Clarendon? Oh you are a sweetheart Drew, but let's be for real."

"Well, I believe you could write like her someday, I mean you can do anything you want. You should let me help you Beth." Drew struggled a bit due to his experience, or lack thereof, with girls. Still he felt he had at least been staying afloat.

"You're really too good to be true Drew, you know that."

"I am serious Beth," Drew wanted to make sure she understood him. He looked her straight in the eyes. "I promise you Beth, I'll be there for you no matter what. You tell me you want my help and neither heaven or hell will keep me from being there for you."

Beth gazed shyly back into his eyes and realized he meant what he'd just said. She moved out of her seat and quickly ascended upon

The Bitter Harvest

Drew to give him a quick kiss on the cheek as she giggled a little and just as quickly sat back in her chair.

Drew was surprised and happy to get this little peck on the cheek as Beth had always been very conservative with her affections towards him. Even after many dates, she had yet to give Drew a kiss on the lips; though he made several attempts and she always reacted as if she wasn't ready yet. He finally decided he wouldn't move too fast for her and mess anything up. He cared too much about her already to do anything that might derail this relationship.

In the hall behind Drew a door opened. This caused Beth to look behind him. Then her eyes opened wide, she let out a little scream and immediately dropped the book to her lap and put her hands up in an effort to cover her eyes. Turning around, Drew saw Rich standing in the doorway with his boxer shorts on and nothing else.

"Oh man, I'm sorry; I didn't know you had company Drew." Rich spoke as if still half asleep.

Drew had completely forgotten about Rich during his campaign to present an acceptable atmosphere for Beth. Yet here Rich stood; with his hair sticking up, a five o'clock shadow and checkered boxer shorts. The sudden appearance of Rich seemed to totally derail his efforts of appearing civilized to Beth. Rich backed out of the doorway and to his room.

"I'm so sorry, that's the roommate I was telling you about." Beth opened her fingers slightly on her right hand exposing her eye.

"Can I lower my hands now?" The words came through her covered face somewhat muffled.

"Yeah, you're as safe as you'll ever be with Rich around." They both laughed.

Rich strolled through the doorway again but this time with sweat pants and a T-shirt on. He raked his hair over with his fingers and then bounced over the couch to land beside Drew. "So Buddy, who's your friend here, she's a real cutie." Rich winked at Beth and her face grimaced just a little, as if to deflect his advance gently.

"Elizabeth Reynolds this is Richard Harrison. My friend since grade school and current roommate," he said waving a hand from Beth to Rich.

"Please call me Rich."

"And you can call me Beth," she said as they shook hands.

"Well, I'm glad to finally meet you Beth. I think you have Drew here stuck on you."

"Come on Rich!" Drew protested, though this was actually something he wanted her to know.

"Really Rich, you don't say!" Beth looked at Drew as if a little suspicious of him and then laughed a bit to ease the tension.

"So Beth, you two going or not? We will be leaving next week with or without you two."

"Going?" She turned to Drew with a puzzled expression and then back to Rich as she shrugged her shoulders. Drew had decided not to mention the trip until a more private setting but again Rich interrupted that plan.

Looking puzzled as he turned directly to Rich, "You mean to tell me you still haven't said anything to her about it?"

"I planned too Rich, but she's only been here a few minutes. And I wish you would have let me bring it up," as he quickly looked at Beth trying to gage her reaction to the information Rich had just blurted out.

"Bring what up? Would someone let me in on the secret?" Beth appeared to not be amused in the least.

"Alaska," Rich blurted out before Drew could say anything. "Do you want to go to Alaska with us? Drew should have asked you already."

"Alaska?" She was perplexed by the whole situation. "What's he talking about Drew?"

"Well, Jack, a friend of ours and his girlfriend Cindy are planning a trip to Alaska. The plan pretty much amounts to the five of us kayaking down one of the rivers; camping and all that outdoors type stuff."

Rich, now seeming content that Drew had spoken to Beth about the plan, bounced off the couch and into the kitchen area directly adjacent to the small living room.

"Hey Drew... did you wash the dishes? Wait, where are the dishes? Drew, did you put the dirty dishes in the oven?" Rolling his eyes and grimacing to the fact Rich now seemed on a mission to sabotage everything; Drew simply decided not to acknowledge his friend.

Beth however, smiled slyly at Drew as if she had just learned something about him she would've never expected. Drew smiled, seeming embarrassed, and shrugged his shoulders indicating he'd been caught.

"Alaska, wow," she said getting back to the conversation at hand. "That all sounds great. But I can't go. I can't possibly afford a trip to Alaska."

"All expenses paid," Rich shouted while his head remained almost entirely inside the refrigerator, but apparently still able to keep up with the conversation. "Hey Drew didn't we have some mustard?"

"Rich, would you let me handle this please, and yes we have some mustard. Wait, what are you eating in the morning that you need mustard for?" forgetting for a brief moment Beth was still sitting across from him.

"All expenses paid? Really Drew?" Beth stared at him as if awaiting a confirmation. Rich meanwhile jumped over the back of the couch in another display of his athletic prowess. This time he had a hot dog in one hand and a can of soda in the other.

"Yeah our friend Jack is paying for it. He's loaded! Tell her Drew," Rich motioned with his elbow since both hands were full.

"Why do I need to tell her anything Rich, you're doing a fine job. And really, hot-dogs for breakfast?"

"Yeah, it's the breakfast of great athletes everywhere," came a muffled reply from a mouth half full of hot dog.

"So how long is this trip going to be for?" She asked. Rich, still eating, started to speak but Drew turned to him with an obviously irritated stare.

"Oh, please go ahead buddy. I'm just trying to help."

Drew turned back to Beth and replied. "It'll only be a few weeks. The weather will start turning bad up in Alaska if we don't go soon. We went to Colorado last year and Wyoming the year before.

Rich had to make up some classes this summer so we didn't think there would be a trip. Then Jack came up with the idea of kayaking down an Alaskan river and as he put it 'exchange a quality trip for quantity trip.'

"Before you make a decision Beth I think you should know this won't be a pleasure cruise. I don't know how you feel about camping, but we'll be sleeping on the ground in small tents and eating packaged meals." Beth thought for a moment, and both guys stared at her in anticipation.

"I think I could handle that," she said after a moment of thought.

"All right then," Rich blurted out. "It's all settled; we are going to Alaska! I'll go tell Jack so we can get the tickets and everything set up." Rich bounced into his room, and a "whoopee" sounded out behind the closed door.

"Beth, you may want to think this over a bit more. Don't let Rich rush you into anything." Drew spoke with a face of concern.

"Well, I think if I'm ever going to write as well as Candace Clarendon I've got to get out in the world and do something. There's no way I could afford to go to Alaska and for me, this seems to be an opportunity I won't often get, if ever again."

Just then Rich came through the door and grabbing his car keys from a change dish in the bookshelf; he went out the door with a quick "see you guys later."

"Yes, I understand that," Drew said getting back to the conversation. "But I think you'll find Jack to be way over confident. He also drinks too much. When we went to Colorado last year, I know of several occasions which flat out frightened me due to his arrogant and somewhat alcohol-induced behavior."

Beth thought about this for a moment. Then she looked at Drew.

"I understand your concern, but as long as you're there, I'll be safe. Surely your competent thoughts can keep things balanced out, right?"

Drew smiled a little. He felt good that Beth thought such a thing about him. He then continued.

"Well, maybe, but other things besides Jack's drinking and over confidence may affect the trip. For example, I've known Rich most of my life, and we've always been great friends. After becoming friends with Jack though he's changed. He doesn't have the money Jack has, but he's beginning to act the way Jack acts. He wants the things Jack has, but I just don't think he'll ever be as successful as Jack. One reason being his family isn't as wealthy as Jack's."

"And did I mention Cindy? Cindy is like Jack in being over confident to the point of arrogance. She also has something of a superiority complex in my opinion. She seems to gravitate towards money and power. Although she's athletic and knows her way around a campsite, she doesn't do any more of the work than necessary.

The gist of it is, you may not be treated as well as you should by her. And I'm suspect of Jack and Rich's abilities with a trip of this scale."

Beth reclined back in her chair as a sail falling when the wind suddenly dies. "So, you think we shouldn't go?" she asked after some thought.

"It's not that I'm saying we shouldn't go. Possibly more along the line of, I don't want you to expect a relaxing vacation. Then the trip turns out to be an exercise of putting up with three somewhat eccentric characters for two weeks. Cindy will most likely not be your best friend and possibly not any friend at all.

Jack thrives on taking things to far in an effort for him appear as some a hero. And Rich has more or less become a student of Jack. Basically, if we go, we should probably go without any unrealistic expectations. If you're all right with that, then I say we should go. But if you're expecting a leisure trip we may need to reconsider."

Beth now appeared to consider what Drew said. Then after a few moments, she seemed to have made a decision.

"I would like to go. I understand your concern, and I respect that you want me to be clear about the trip, but I don't think I'm as fragile as people may think. I'm really frightened I'll be upset with myself later if I pass the opportunity simply because of possible challenges."

Drew didn't get surprised at the decision. He suspected she would want to go but wanted to be sure she understood the circumstances.

"All right then, we'll go." He relaxed a bit now that she understood what they might be in for and a decision had been made.

"I suppose I should get ready then." Beth said with some excitement.

Yeah, that is probably a good idea." Drew said. "I'll let you know when we'll be leaving, as soon as I hear from Jack or Rich. I'll also make sure to reserve us a nice roomy tent if possible." Drew smiled with the best suave, male type smile he could muster.

"Hey now, don't get any ideas," Beth moved back a bit into her chair, "you know I'm not that type of girl Drew." She had a very firm voice but smiled a little. Drew immediately tried to fix any possible damage.

"Oh yeah, I know that Beth, separate tents, I was just kidding around."

"I'll call you Monday to check in," she said rising from her chair, leaning over giving Drew another little peck on the cheek before she walked to the door, opened it and left quietly. The kiss didn't exactly meet his hoped for expectations, but after the intense experience with Rich, he considered this another small step in the right direction.

Chapter Two: Whisper

The following week everything had been set up for the trip. Beth called Drew several times throughout the week and he would relay the plan. Thursday morning she arrived at his door, smiling as usual and prepared to fly out that afternoon.

"Is that all the luggage you have?" Drew stared at her large denim shoulder bag and single small suitcase. She glanced down at her baggage.

"All expenses paid right?"

"Yeah, I just thought you being a woman…"

Beth gave him a glaring stare when he said this.

"Oh, never mind," Drew said, in an attempt to not put his foot any further into his mouth.

From the apartment they took a taxi to the airport and got onto a plane. Beth held onto Drew as the plane left the ground.

"Are you all right?" He asked her as she squeezed his arm.

"I've never flown before." She replied with a frightened tone in her voice.

"You should have told me," he said with a slight chuckle. He then took her other hand and held it as the plane climbed high into the air.

Once the plane reached cruising altitude Beth calmed down. Jack ordered a drink and Rich followed Jack's lead, soon ordering a drink as well.

Drew hoped Cindy might begin to socialize with Beth on the plane but instead Cindy also soon had a drink in hand and paid no attention to Beth who sat across the aisle from her.

He did come to enjoy the take off and landings of the flights. He would hold Beth's hand and she held his arm tightly.

Since Cindy ignored Beth for the most part, Drew focused on keeping her company. When he wasn't talking to her she would pull her Candace Clarendon book out and read quietly.

After several flights the group found themselves walking down mobile stairs in order to depart their plane at the Fairbanks Alaska airport. The airport seemed a bit old-fashioned and out of date, but Jack, having indulged in a number of drinks; on as well as off the planes, reveled in the atmosphere.

"Now we're in the wild," he exclaimed loudly as he walked down the stairs, holding his arms up and presenting the small airport and the obvious wilderness in the background to his fellow companions.

Drew thought he'd packed modestly but as he examined Beth's small amount of baggage he felt a bit embarrassed that his luggage required two hands to carry rather than one arm.

Once inside the airport, Jack made a call from a pay phone and directly a small van taxi picked them up and off they went.

The hotel they arrived at certainly wouldn't be considered five star accommodations, but Drew realized in the wilderness setting of Fairbanks it would be sufficient. Also, this must be the best available since Jack had paid.

The following day Jack moved from room to room getting everyone up and around. He seemed to thrive on being a boss. Drew actually thought of him as being bossy on these trips rather than being much of an actual leader. Jack just told everyone what to do without much thought or more often than not with an alcohol induced thought behind it. As the benefactor for these trips however, Jack assumed total control and this fact often concerned Drew.

Putting his glasses on, Drew stepped into the hall followed by Rich. Soon Beth stepped out of her room. He admired Beth in her shorts and tiny tee shirt. Strange, he thought, even this early in the morning she almost glowed. Maybe he was falling in love; he turned away before she noticed him watching her.

The warm feeling Drew had about Beth concerned him some. As he got ready, he thought about it. He'd never been in love before. Even in high school he was the guy who simply fell flat on his face when dealing with girls. His failed attempts to flirt with the young women he'd liked in high school echoed in his mind like sad songs, long overplayed.

Now the feeling he had for Beth was like a warm fire inside his heart. He wouldn't let anything harm this wonderful relationship developing between them. This was something special and he would treat it as a delicate flower that he must tend to gently and patiently.

After a quick breakfast the group moved outside and found a large van waiting. Three brand new, bright red, double seated kayaks sat on a trailer connected to the van. After some admiring and touching of the new kayaks, the group began loading their bags in the vehicle. Jack spoke with the driver and loaded his bag last. After a short drive they arrived at an outfitting store.

"All right gang," Jack instantly took the lead role, "here is a list of stuff we must have and if you think of anything else, go ahead and get it. However, keep in mind there's not much room in a kayak."

Inside the store everyone rounded up sleeping bags, tents , etc. One of the items on the list Drew and Beth received was 'one hundred feet of nylon rope.'

Drew moved over to Beth as she admired a light blue coat.

"You may need that." He said.

Beth smiled.

"I didn't bring much money, so I'll do without."

He took the jacket from her hand and examined the front, and back; then he held it up to Beth.

The Bitter Harvest

"Yes, I'm absolutely sure now," he said.

"Sure of what?"

"This coat, I noticed as I held it up to you, no one else would be as beautiful in it as you would." When he said this Beth laughed a little and this made Drew smile also.

"Well, I'm not going to ask Jack to spend anymore money on me. I don't want to take advantage of him."

Drew gave her a silly face. "No, no, I certainly don't want you to take advantage of Jack. In fact I'm going to buy some things for you just to make sure if anyone gets taken advantage of by you, it'll be me! Call me crazy Beth, but I kind of enjoy the thought of you taking advantage of me."

Beth gave him the sad smile he loved, then laughed as Drew laughed along with her.

"Hey, what's going on over there?" Rich shouted from several racks over.

"I'm working on a method for Beth to take advantage of me," Drew replied with some excitement.

"Oh, well never mind, forget I asked," Rich walked in the opposite direction and this caused Beth and Drew to laugh even more.

Drew found a coat his size; similar to the one she'd picked out and soon everyone gathered together outside, ready to go. The group loaded into the van and off they went again.

As they drove out of Fairbanks the wilderness closed in around them. Soon moose could be spotted from time to time grazing on the side of the road. Rich seemed to almost jump out of the window when he spotted a black bear with several young bears in tow.

After several hours of driving, the van pulled off the highway and up to several log buildings. Two older style gas pumps stood outside and a sign over the larger of the two buildings read "Eagle Ridge

Trading Post." About twenty yards behind the buildings a river could be seen. The group got out of the van; looked around and stretched.

In front of the trading post the parking area fairly well amounted to rock, gravel and some random mud holes. Trees and brush embraced the isolated speck of humanity. The driver of the van started backing the trailer down the brushy trail to the river once everyone had disembarked.

"Last stop before the river run," Jack said, seeming to be energized now that danger permeated the atmosphere. He continued, "If you want or need anything else, such as feminine unmentionables or such, this would be the place to take care of that."

"Let's go browse a bit shall we?" Drew said to Beth. She nodded. Together they walked up to the trading post. As they entered the door an old fashioned doorbell connected to the top rang out.

The aroma inside consisted of cut wood, a wood stove and a variety of foods, meats, leathers and several smells that Drew couldn't quite identify. He realized this must be an old establishment yet it was well built.

As the two progressed through the store they passed souvenir T-shirts, coats, hats and other Alaska items. On the opposite side of a checkout counter was an elderly lady, but she stood tall and seemed to be very fit despite her apparent age.

Behind the woman, on the wall, hung a number of antique items such as snowshoes, and a harpoon as well as some harpoon tips that appeared to be fashioned from bone. In between the large array of Alaskan artifacts stood a shelf and on this shelf rested many smaller assorted artifacts, all arranged neatly for display.

Beth gazed at the items with interest; her mouth slightly open as if the shiny trinkets held her spellbound. Drew glanced over at her and immediately thought of a child examining the flavor list on the side of an ice cream truck.

The Bitter Harvest

He then followed an invisible line from her eyes, to identify which item had captured so much attention from her. On a center shelf, in the middle of the various antiques, stood a small red bottle with what looked to be faded ivory decorations around the outside.

While this took place the elderly lady moved to the end of the counter to do what Drew would call busy work.

"You kids are going out on the river a little late in the year aren't you?" The woman seemed to be asking though she never looked up from her dusting and organizing.

"Yes, I suppose we are," Drew replied as he moved closer to Beth. Then a thought occurred to him while standing beside her.

"Excuse me, could we see the little red bottle on the middle shelf?" When Drew asked the lady this Beth seemed to awaken from her trance.

"What are you doing?" She spoke in a whisper and as if a bit embarrassed by his request. The woman came over to the counter and picked up the bottle, then handed it to Drew. He held the bottle in his hand for a few seconds and noticed Beth's eyes light up. She moved very close to him as he examined the delicate item.

"What a beautiful little bottle," was all she said.

The small glass container had a deep, almost glowing red color. What appeared to be faded ivory had been fashioned on the outside and the distinct outline of a tiger or large cat could be made out around it in a delicate fashion.

Drew thought the ivory must surely have been hand carved and the bottle itself certainly very old.

"That particular bottle is an antique Chinese snuff bottle, from what I've been told over the years. Supposedly it came from Whisper," the old woman said as she watched them admiring it.

"Whisper?" Beth turned to the old woman with an apparent lack of understanding.

"Yes, Whisper. It's something of an Atlantis in these parts. Some people think the place really exists and others say the story is another Alaskan tall tale from the gold rush days.

"That little bottle I received as a gift from my uncle around, oh, maybe twenty years ago. He worked for the forestry service and according to him a hiker stumbled out of the woods almost half dead. He gave it to my uncle after telling him the bottle had come from Whisper."

"So, is Whisper a town or...?" Drew asked, becoming very interested by this time.

"I suppose we would call it a town, but then we call a congregation of ten people and five dogs a town around here," the woman said smiling.

"The story, from what I've heard goes this way. Back during the gold rush days two brothers by the name of Janik and Felix Varga came to Alaska searching for gold. No one really noticed when they arrived as they came along with hundreds of others. How long the two struggled in the Alaskan wild is also unknown.

"They turned up one day in Fairbanks, straight from the wilderness, carrying with them almost pure gold nuggets, some of which they promptly sold for tickets back to the States. This is, of course when they became noticed.

"Most of the people that did take notice however had forgotten about the brothers or moved on by the following spring when the two returned to Fairbanks. But, a few remembered the gold nuggets they possessed the previous year and decided to follow them to locate the rich find.

"The brothers must have been aware of this possibility and put a plan together. They rented an old store building on the edge of town. Over the next several weeks their family and close associates arrived in Fairbanks five and ten at a time.

"The activity around the old store building picked up as the people connected to the Varga group arrived. It wasn't long before a small group of swindlers desiring to find the brothers gold began to keep an eye on the group.

"First they tried to get information from people in the group. None of the party said anything however, and for the most part they would aggressively brush off the 'would be' claim jumpers.

"Some of the spies tried to follow the brothers in an effort to locate the mysterious location. The Varga brothers must have also foreseen this though as they would separate and move about at all hours of the day and night. They slyly evaded their pursuers again and again. During this time people began to speculate, and as the Varga group grew larger and became more elusive in their affairs, a kind of pre-legend began to grow around them. I don't suspect anyone at that time foresaw what was about to happen.

"After weeks of continual activity around the old rented store building; someone noticed the Varga group had vanished. All the people desiring to horn in on the brothers gold were sorely disappointed when they arrived at the old store building to find the tents still up but not a soul to be found.

"The consensus eventually came down to two theories concerning their disappearance. The first theory was that the group had a preset date to move. Then, possibly during a brief night, they all moved quickly from Fairbanks and no one noticed.

"The second theory and the one that seems most likely, is that small groups left until only a few were around. These few went about tending numerous campfires and creating the impression of there still being a large group at the store building. Then this small group slipped away at a convenient moment."

At this point the woman had to stop and tend a customer. After a moment she returned. Drew and Beth stared at her intently. She appeared to be having trouble recalling her thoughts. Then she asked.

"So where was I?"

Beth replied quickly.

"The Varga group vanished from Fairbanks."

"Oh yeah, that is correct." The woman said, as she re-established her train of thought.

"So anyway, the entire Varga operation looked to be a complete success at first. Everyone seemed to have been totally surprised by the Varga's ability to keep complete secrecy.

"Then, finally, after a week or so of absolute darkness on the matter, a young boy surfaced to shed a little bit of light on the group's disappearance.

"This young boy as it turns out, had been playing with one of the Varga brother's nieces. She made him promise not to tell anyone before she would reveal anything to him. And it was with some reluctance that the young lad gave any information.

"When he did finally speak on the matter, he said the young girl told him she and the others were moving to a secret location her uncles had found for them. Once there, they would build a town. Her uncles had already named the town Whisper. She also informed the boy that everyone in the town would become rich."

At this point the woman stopped. Drew and Beth both stared at her in anticipation.

"So what happened?" Drew finally asked.

"No one knows," she said as if she had been looking for another starting point. "The Varga group disappeared into the wilderness of Alaska and no one knows what happened to them."

"Didn't anyone look for them?" Beth asked.

The Bitter Harvest

"Sure they did, in fact a few years later some relatives of the people who left with the brothers sent detectives and scouts to search for their loved ones.

"As a result of these inquiries and an investigation by local authorities, a gold stake claim surfaced which the Varga brothers filed before leaving. But when the area of this claim was searched, the result came to nothing but open wilderness. A theory came to be that either the brothers simply filed a worthless claim to throw off any pursuers or they were confused themselves as to the exact location according to a map."

"So, everyone just gave up looking for them?" Drew asked with a bit of disbelief.

The woman took a slow deep breath before continuing. "No not really; actually there's been people looking for Whisper ever since the Varga group showed up with the gold nuggets. And many of them have just disappeared as well. No one knows how many explorers and gold hunters have vanished in the Alaskan wilderness while searching for Whisper.

"You should also keep in mind the time frame we're talking about. When the Varga group disappeared, Alaska could only be searched by ground and maybe to some extent by river. With the sheer size involved, any search would be difficult as well as possibly deadly for searchers.

"This isn't your average wilderness and you kids should get your little canoe trip wrapped up before the snow starts. I strongly suggest you get back into civilization within a couple of weeks. If the snow comes early you could get into real trouble."

"Yes, we plan on being out a few weeks and no more," Drew said, and then after a slight pause continued.

"I wonder if you would be interested in selling this bottle."

The old woman looked at Drew a little strangely.

"Well, young man, everything in this building is for sale, but you should know, I'm quite fond of that little bottle."

"That is fair warning. Let's talk about price."

Drew and the woman negotiated for a while, but eventually he got the bottle.

"I can't believe what you paid for that bottle," Beth exclaimed as they walked out the door. "You must have really wanted it."

"As a matter of fact I did," Drew said with a sly tone. He stopped and Beth stopped. "I wanted to get you something very special Beth and that jacket is not nearly special enough. I bought the bottle for you."

Drew handed the small sack with the bottle to Beth. She took the small package and clasped it in her hands as if it were a kitten or small treasure. Several tears immediately began welling up in her eyes and she turned her head down to avoid Drew seeing her cry.

"No one has ever done anything like this for me." She said, trying to speak through the tears.

Drew gently lifted her head with his hand under her chin. He gazed into her eyes and then wiped a tear from her cheek. She smiled and then laughed and almost cried at the same time.

"Come on now, a beautiful girl like you, I find that a little hard to believe. But at least I know now this is the special something I've been looking for, and that's a good thing." He said softly as she hugged the small sack.

"Beth, I want to do more than just buy you a present." As Drew said this Beth became serious and gazed into his eyes. Realizing he wanted to tell her something special she listened closely.

"I want to be the man that changes everything for you. I want to be the man you can count on; the one that will be there when you need me to be there. Beth, I promise you here and now that I'll be there for you when you need me. I won't ever let you down."

He paused for a few seconds and Beth wrapped her arms around him in an embrace. Drew ran his hand over her brown hair and continued.

"In fact, when we get back I would like for you to get an apartment closer to me. In the same complex if possible; I'd feel better. I'll help you with the finances. I really want you to be closer and, well, I would just feel better."

Beth looked up at him. She studied his face for a few seconds and put her head back on his chest.

"I just don't know if I'm ready for that Drew. I know you're concerned. I'll think about it, all right?" She again looked up to him. Drew nodded to her.

She then gave Drew a quick kiss on the lips. She pulled the bottle from the sack and admired it briefly. Drew smiled as she appeared happy. She then put the small bottle into a pocket of the jacket he'd bought for her earlier.

Drew felt a flash of excitement run through his body from head to toe. He was now glad they came on the trip.

As the two walked arm in arm to the river they could see Jack and Cindy standing beside the van talking. Rich busily packed the front of his two man kayak with supplies.

"Come on you two love birds, we need to get on the water," Jack yelled out as he pulled a map from his pocket.

Drew felt flush with confidence after his success with Beth.

As they came closer Drew said. "Before we get on the water, could you please tell us the plan?"

Jack turned to him, expressing some surprise at this type of remark coming from Drew.

"Well, my good man, and fair lady, the plan is quite simple." Jack unfolded the map across the hood and windshield of the van. "We simply get on the river right here, and travel straight down to Jackson Point right there."

After Jack said this, Cindy, rather snidely, commented. "There's nothing simpler than that." She then strolled off towards the kayaks with a few small items in her hands.

Drew, not quite as impressed as Cindy, took a closer look at the map.

"Yeah, I see the river runs down to Jackson Point, but what about all of these branches in the river, if we get on one of those we'll end up out in the middle of the Alaskan wilderness."

Jack smiled at Drew, as if he had just called him on a poker hand.

"That's a sharp observation Drew, but if you'll notice, as long as we stay alert and always stay to the right and not venture off on any of the left forks, we'll remain on the major river run."

Drew and Beth studied the map a few seconds.

"Okay," Drew replied, "I see you've got a thought out plan, that's all I needed to know."

Jack flashed an arrogant smile, folded up the map and then walked up to the trading post as Drew and Beth packed gear into their kayak.

The driver moved the van away from the river and the group waited for Jack.

Soon he could be seen heading back towards the river, stumbling a bit as if he'd been drinking a bit too much already. He had a bag cradled in his left arm.

He stopped and talked with the driver of the van for a few moments. Then came on down to the river as the van pulled away.

Everyone watched Jack as he tried to put the bag into him and Cindy's kayak. There wasn't enough room. He came over to Drew and Beth.

"Put this in your kayak would you?"

Drew could hear the glass bottles inside the bag and knew the contents must be some type of booze.

"We don't have room Jack." Though Drew didn't want to take the booze at all, he did speak the truth about not having room.

"Nonsense," Jack dug around in the kayak and pulled out a bag. "What's this?"

Drew looked at the bag. "That's a hundred feet of nylon rope."

Jack threw the bag up on the river bank.

"After some thought, I've realized this rope won't be required after all." He then put the bag in the spot where the rope had been. "All right, let's move out," he said and moved over to his kayak.

Thank you for reading the Tears of Abandon preview. I hope you enjoyed it. Please check out all of Oliver Phipps' books online. For your convenience I've listed a few Oliver Phipps books you may also be interested in.

Oliver Phipps

Twelve Minutes till Midnight

A man catches a ride on a dusty Louisiana road only to find out he's traveling with notorious outlaws Bonnie and Clyde.

The suspense is nonstop as confrontation settles in between a man determined to stand on truth and an outlaw determined to dislocate him from it.

"Twelve Minutes till Midnight will take you on an unforgettable ride."

Ghosts of Company K

Tag along with young Bud Fisher during his daily adventures in this ghostly tale based on actual events. It's 1971 and Bud and his family move into an old house in Northern Arkansas. Bud soon discovers they live not far from a very interesting cave as well as a historic Civil War battle site. As odd things start to happen, Bud tries to solve the mysteries. But soon the entire family experiences a haunting situation.

If you enjoy ghost tales based on true events, then you'll enjoy Ghosts of Company K. This heartwarming story brings the reader into the life and experiences of a young boy growing up in the early 1970s. Seen through innocent and unsuspecting eyes, Ghosts of Company K reveals a haunting tale from the often unseen perspective of a young boy.

Oliver Phipps

Diver Creed Station

Wars, disease and a massive collapse of civilization have ravaged the human race of a hundred years in the future. Finally, in the late twenty- second century, humanity slowly begins to struggle back from the edge of extinction.

When a huge "virtual life" facility is restored from a hibernation type of storage and slowly brought back online, a new hope materializes.

Fragments of humanity begin to move into the remnants of Denver and the Virtua-Gauge facilities, which offer seven days of virtual leisure for seven days work in this new and growing social structure.

Most inhabitants of this new lifestyle begin to hate the real world and work for the seven day period inside the virtual pods. It's the variety of luxury role play inside the virtual zone that supply's the incentive needed to work hard for seven days in the real world.

In this new social structure, a man can work for seven days in a food dispersal unit and earn seven days as a twenty-first century software billionaire in the virtual zone. As time goes by and more of the virtual pods are brought back online life appears to be getting better.

Rizette and her husband Oray are young technicians that settle into their still new marriage as the virtual facilities expand and thrive.

Oray has recently attained the level of a Class A Diver and enjoys his job. The Divers are skilled technicians that perform critical repairs to the complex system, from inside the virtual zone.

The Bitter Harvest

His title of Diver originates from often working in the secure "lower levels" of the system. These lower level areas are the dividing space between the real world and the world of the virtual zone. When the facility was built, the original designers intentionally placed this buffer zone in the system to avoid threats from non-living virtual personnel.

As Oray becomes more experienced in his elite technical position as a Diver, he's approached by his virtual assistant and forced to make a difficult decision. Oray's decision triggers events that soon pull him and his wife Rizette into a deadly quest for survival.

The stage becomes a massive and complex maze of virtual world sequences as escape or entrapment hang on precious threads of information.

System ghosts from the distant past intermingle with mysterious factions that have thrown Oray and Rizette into a cyberspace trap with little hope for survival.

Oliver Phipps

Where the Strangers Live

When a passenger plane disappeared over the Indian Ocean in autumn 2013, a massive search gets underway.

A deep trolling, unmanned pod picks up faint readings and soon the deep sea submersible Oceana and her three crew members are four miles below the ocean surface in search of the black box from flight N340.

Nothing could have prepared the submersible crew for what they discover and what happens afterward. Ancient evils and other world creatures challenge the survival of the Oceana's crew. Secrets of the past are revealed, but death hangs in the balance for Sophie, Troy and Eliot in this deep sea Science Fiction thriller.

The House on Cooper Lane

It's 1984 and all Bud Fisher wants to do is find a place to live in Madison Louisiana. With his dog Badger, they come across a beautiful old mansion that was converted into apartments.

Something should have felt odd when he found out nobody lived in the apartments. To make matters worse, the owner is reluctant to let him rent one. Eventually, he negotiates an apartment in the old historic house but soon finds out that he's not quite as alone as he thought. What ghostly secret has the owner failed to share?

It's up to Bud to unravel the mysteries of the upstairs apartments, but is he ready to find out the truth?

Bane of the Innocent

"There's no reason for them to shoot us; we ain't anyone" - Sammy, Bane of the Innocent.

Two young boys become unlikely companions during the fall of Atlanta. Sammy and Ben somehow find themselves, and each other, in the rapidly changing and chaotic environment of the war-torn Georgia City.

As the siege ends and the fall begins in late August and early September of 1864 the Confederate troops begin to move out, and Union forces cautiously move into the city. Ben and Sammy simply struggle to survive, but in the process, they develop a friendship that will prove more important than either one could imagine.

CPSIA information can be obtained
at www.ICGtesting.com
Printed in the USA
LVHW09s1017220918
591047LV00001B/145/P